THE SEER

Witch Ball

LINDA JOY SINGLETON

Llewellyn Publications
Woodbury, Minnesota

First Edition
First printing, 2006

Cover design and witch ball illustration by Lisa Novak
Editing by Rhiannon Ross

Llewellyn is a registered trademark of Llewellyn Worldwide, Ltd.

Library of Congress Cataloging-in-Publication Data
(Pending)
ISBN 13: 987-0-7387-0821-8
ISBN 10: 0-7387-0821-6

Llewellyn Publications
A Division of Llewellyn Worldwide, Ltd.
2143 Wooddale Drive, Dept. 0-7387-0821-6
Woodbury, MN 55125-2989, U.S.A.
www.llewellyn.com

Printed in the United States of America

Coming soon from Linda Joy Singleton

The Seer #4, *Sword Play*

To Linda Burns,
a special Phantom Friend who shares
my loves of series books and reality shows.

1

"Come on Sabine, dish!" Penny-Love said as the cheerleaders closed in on me around the table. "How was your big weekend? Did Josh like your parents? Did they like him? Did you and Josh sneak off to your old bedroom?"

Everyone giggled, and I blushed. When Penny-Love invited me to join her and a few other cheerleaders at Pepper's Pizza after school, I'd thought they'd discuss plans for the Booster Club Carnival. I hadn't known my love life was on the menu. Leave it to the Queen of Gossip to turn my twin sisters' birthday into a wild party.

"No," I told her firmly. "Josh did *not* see my bedroom."

"What *exactly* did he see?"

"Nothing."

Penny-Love flipped back her curly, red hair as she turned to the other girls. "Anyone who believes that, raise your hand."

I looked around for support, but Jill, Catelyn, and Kaitlyn were hands-down behind Penny-Love. They sipped sodas and leaned closer, obviously not wanting to miss a juicy word. For a moment, I felt panicked—like a cornered rabbit surrounded by hunters. I glanced at the pizza counter, hoping our orders would arrive and I would be saved from answering. But then I realized something that calmed me. This was *exactly* what I'd wanted—to be accepted, even admired, by popular friends. Since starting a new high school, I'd worked hard to fit in like I was normal. Talking about my love life was a small price to pay.

"It was just a birthday party for my sisters," I said with a shrug. "It was held at an amusement park, then afterwards a few of us went back to the house to watch my sisters open their presents. Josh was nice enough to go with me."

"Did he get to unwrap anything?" Penny-Love asked with a sly wink.

"No!" I swatted her on the arm. "You are sooo bad."

"It's a gift," she teased.

Everyone giggled, and I managed to smile even though the word "gift" made me cringe. If my friends knew about my gift of psychic visions, they'd think I was a freak. After what happened at my last school, I was more careful now.

So I told them all the good stuff about Josh; how he arrived early because he wanted to stop somewhere romantic on the way and how he gave me a chocolate kiss, then when it melted in my mouth, his lips melted on my lips. Everyone oohed and wanted details, but I kept it PG 13, not that there were any R moments. Josh wasn't that kind of guy. In fact, he had such a high code of ethics, I found myself watching what I said around him. There were things he didn't need to know.

The pizzas arrived and I reached for a slice smothered in mushrooms and pepperoni. Steamy cheese and tomato smells wafted around us as we gave up talking for eating. But after a few minutes, I noticed that Jill was staring at a notebook and hardly touching her pizza.

Jill lifted her head and tapped her fork against the table. "Everyone, listen up." she said in her most serious squad captain tone. "You know why I called this emergency meeting."

I raised my brows. No, I didn't know. Penny-Love hadn't mentioned any emergency. Did she have an ulterior motive for inviting me? I shot her a suspicious look—which she ignored.

"The carnival is in two days and we have major problems. Here's my to-do list." Jill pushed her plate aside and flipped open the notebook. She was always making lists and was respected for being a take-charge leader who could order people around without coming off bitchy. "We still need makeup for the face-painting booth, a teacher volunteer for the 'Dunk the Teacher' booth, and we have to fill three empty booths. Any ideas?"

"I vote we dunk my algebra teacher," Kaitlyn joked. She had a quirky sense of humor, the opposite of her studious best friend Catelyn.

"I'd rather dunk Mr. Blankenship," Penny-Love said. "His awful ties and polyester suits are a crime; he deserves to get dunked."

"Instead of a teacher, how about Principal Cowboy?" Catelyn suggested. "He's got a good sense of humor and might do it."

I wasn't a cheerleader—more of a mascot, as Penny-Love teased—so I didn't join in. I listened without saying anything and found myself drifting above it all, watching the scene. Only I hardly recognized myself. The girl who was me looked happy, as if she fit in this cozy group of great hair, greater bodies, and popularity-plus. To my friends, my life probably seemed perfect. I earned good grades, I was on the school newspaper, and I had a sizzling hot boyfriend. Penny-Love was always complaining about her rowdy brothers and strict parents, and thought I had it easy living with my grandmother.

She was both right and wrong. Living with Nona was great, but it hadn't been my idea. After a scandal at my old school because I'd predicted the death of a star athlete, my mother kicked me out. For months we hadn't spoken. She hadn't even wanted me to attend my own sisters' party, but I'd gone anyway, and instead of a disaster, things went surprisingly well. Mom was impressed with Josh and seemed almost comfortable with me.

"So how about it, Sabine?" Jill was asking.

I looked up with a start and found everyone staring at me like I had pizza sauce on my nose. I wiped my hand across my face.

"Will you talk to Manny for us?" Jill said.

"Uh . . . sure." I paused. "About what?"

"The fortune-telling booth. Didn't you hear anything I just said?" When I shrugged sheepishly, Jill explained. "Penny-Love says you're really tight with Manny DeVries, and he amazes everyone with his Mystic Manny school newspaper column, so he'd make a fantastic fortune-teller at our carnival. Think he'd do it?"

I glanced over at Penny-Love sharply. Had she set me up? But I kept my unease to myself and shrugged like it wasn't a big deal. "There's no predicting what Manny will do."

"Will you ask him?" Jill persisted with a smile that was hard to refuse.

"Come on, Sabine," Penny-Love pleaded. "Ask him for us."

"Sure. I'll talk to him at school tomorrow, but no guarantees."

"Great!" Everyone smiled at me, and I felt lucky to be part of this fun group. I didn't want to disappoint them, and hoped Manny would say yes. He was a complex mix of ego, honesty, and ambition.

He thrived on being unconventional and was respected for his fearless attitude. He'd proven himself a trusted friend, and was one of only two people at school who knew I was psychic.

More plans for booths were made, while pizza slices disappeared and drinks were refilled. Talk shifted to Penny-Love (as usual) and she told everyone about how my grandmother planned to hire her as a "Love" assistant. Nona ran a computer dating service called Soul Mate Matches, but a serious health condition had recently caused her to need an assistant. I worried about my grandmother and had recently bought a cell phone so she could contact me if she was in trouble.

So when my phone rang, I dropped my pizza.

It was Nona—and she sounded frantic.

"Hurry home!" she cried. "It's the witch ball!"

2

I hid my anxiety from my friends, saying I had to leave because my grandmother needed help defrosting the freezer. It was a lame excuse, but Penny-Love would have insisted on coming along for anything but a housework emergency. I did not want the Queen of Gossip to know about the weird side of my life.

As I pedaled home on my bike, my mind spun faster than my legs. Nona had sounded so fright-

8

ened, worse than when her memory failed and she couldn't find car keys or important papers. Despite her worsening illness, she always remained upbeat and confident. I was usually the one who leaned on her. So having her call in a panic was really unnerving. What had she meant by her cryptic message?

The witch ball.

A distant relative had given it to me over a week ago. The sphere sparkled with rainbow-tinted crystal shards trapped inside clear glass. It was so pretty, obviously a rare antique, and I'd been excited to show it to Nona. But instead of being impressed, she'd ordered me to "get that cursed thing out of my sight!"

"Cursed?" I'd asked in astonishment. "You can't be serious. It's just a glass ball."

"A *witch* ball," she'd corrected.

I was totally baffled by Nona's reaction and wondered if paranoia was another symptom of her illness. Sure the ball gave off strange vibes, but that's what made it fascinating. Antiques often carried energy from the past—the older they were—the stronger the energy. From the moment I held the ball, I'd been intrigued by the strange aura I sensed within its depth.

Out of curiosity last week, I'd looked up "witch ball" on the Internet. Despite the spooky name, there was nothing magical about the glass balls. According to legend, centuries ago witch balls were hung in windows to ward off evil from passing witches. Any negative thoughts were supposed to reflect back to the sender. While I believed in ghosts and spirits, I didn't believe in old-fashioned superstitions. I liked to pet black cats and thirteen was my favorite number. Still, to pacify my grandmother, I'd shut the ball inside my closet.

So why had she made the frantic call?

A car honked as I pedaled onto Lincoln Avenue. It never took long to ride my bike anywhere in semi-rural Sheridan Valley. But now the short mile back to my home seemed like a cross-country trip.

Autumn trees, golden-brown fields, and houses blurred as I neared Lilac Lane. There were fewer homes on this rural road, bordered by tangled woods that stretched to Nona's ten-acre farm. Passing our barn-shaped mailbox, I careened into the long dirt driveway. Gravel and dust kicked up as my wheels churned, and through oak trees I saw Nona's weathered yellow farmhouse. It looked so peaceful, and I felt a comforting sense of belonging. Home was no longer in San Jose with my parents, but here in the heart of Nona's farm, and I was terrified of losing it all.

As I neared the house, I saw my grandmother on the porch—only she wasn't alone. Dominic stood beside her. Part handyman and part apprentice to Nona, Dominic was still a mystery to me. He seemed a few years older than me, but he didn't go to school or discuss his past. All I knew was that his mother had died, he'd suffered abuse from a cruel uncle, and had an unusual connection to animals.

As usual, his sandy brown hair waved out of place and he wore rugged jeans and western boots. He was leaning close to Nona protectively, but when he turned toward me, his blue eyes hardened like stone.

"About time." Typical Dominic—short on words but high on attitude.

"I left as soon as Nona called." I dropped my bike and rushed up the porch steps. "Nona, are you okay?"

"Yes." Loose silver-brown tendrils of hair escaped from her paisley scarf and she pushed them back as she offered a weak smile. "I-I suppose I overreacted. It was just such a shock seeing . . ."

"Seeing what?" I put my arm around her shoulders and was surprised to find her trembling.

Dominic pursed his lips. "You should know."

"Well, I don't," I said breathlessly, and not only because I'd raced here on my bike. I couldn't understand why Dominic was acting so hostile to me, which added to the tension between us since our trip to Pine Peaks. We'd gotten intimate in an unexpected moment, and now everything was awkward. I didn't know what he thought or if he wondered what I thought or if I even cared. It was safer to keep my distance, which I had—until now.

"You brought it here," Dominic told me, "so you're responsible."

"For what?"

"Putting that up there," Nona answered, pointing high at the kitchen window. Her face was so pale, the wrinkles stood out, as if she'd aged twenty years since I'd left for school this morning.

I followed her gaze and saw rainbow lights flash in the window. "Is that the witch ball?" I murmured, puzzled. "Who hung it up there?"

"You?" Dominic guessed.

"No way! I left it in my closet."

"It didn't stay there." Nona sank on the porch swing.

"Very strange." Dominic ran his rugged hand over his forehead. When he moved closer to me, his nearness made my breath catch. Neither of us said anything. I wondered if he was thinking about the witch ball or remembering that stormy night when a surreal moment on a dance floor led to our kissing.

I stepped back from him. "I don't know how the witch ball got into the kitchen. It's been in my closet since Nona asked me to put it away. Someone must have taken it from my room."

"Or it moved by itself," my grandmother said in a hushed tone, rocking slightly on the swing, her hands clasped in her lap.

"Impossible," I insisted.

Dominic touched his chin thoughtfully. "The animals *have* been acting strange. Keeping away from the house."

"You can't possibly think the witch ball is haunted."

His blue eyes darkened as he leaned closer to me. "What do *you* think?"

The questions in his gaze made my heart jump. Were we still talking about the witch ball? I gave a firm shake of my head. "It's not haunted."

"Are you sure?"

"I haven't seen any visions or ghosts."

"So who moved the ball?"

"I have no idea," I said a bit defensively. "I've been at school, and then at the pizza parlor—"

"With your boyfriend?" Dominic asked with a frown.

"No. I was with Penny-Love and some friends." I felt my cheeks heat up and wondered why he was even asking. He couldn't possibly care whom I went out with. He probably didn't even remember our kiss. If only I could forget . . .

I moved away from him and sat beside Nona on the porch swing, gently taking her hand in mine. "I'm sorry the ball upset you."

"It's evil." Nona stared up at the window. "I refuse to go inside until it's gone."

"I offered to get rid of it," Dominic said, "but Nona wouldn't let me."

"Not without first talking to Sabine." She turned back to me. "I was hoping you'd have a logical explanation."

"I wish I did—but I don't. I'll go take it down."

When I entered the kitchen, I stared up, amazed all over again by the glass ball's beauty. Dazzling colors reflected from the glittery sphere, dancing across the walls like a rainbow ballet. The ball dangled over the sink, hung from a string loped over a nail. Despite its witchy name, it certainly hadn't hopped on a broom and flown to the kitchen window. So how *did* it get up there?

There was one explanation I didn't want to consider, but sadly it made the most sense. Had Nona moved the ball herself and then forgotten? Her failing memory caused her to behave strangely; a few weeks ago she'd left the house for a luncheon, wearing her nightgown and slippers. Fortunately, I'd stopped her before she'd gotten too far.

I pushed a chair over by the window, then climbed high to reach the witch ball. It seemed so happy in the window, as if it belonged in sunlight, and I felt oddly guilty for taking it down. But I didn't want to upset Nona any further. Unhooking the ball, I carried it back into my bedroom.

"Is Nona right?" I murmured, turning the glass ball between my hands as I sat on the edge of my bed. "Are you haunted?"

It's not going to answer, a sassy voice spoke in my mind.

"Hey, Opal," I greeted my spirit guide. Opal was my go-between with the other side. She could be really bossy, but I could usually trust whatever she told me. So I asked her about the witch ball.

You do manage to connect yourself to the unusual, she told me and my mind-vision of her was smiling with amusement. *I cease to understand why you call upon me to solve all your trivial concerns.*

"Just tell me yes or no . . . is this witch ball haunted?"

To simply put it—since you insist of a blunt manner of speaking—maybe.

"Maybe! What kind of answer is that?"

A true answer.

"Is there a ghost inside the ball?"

Ghosts do not reside within earthly objects. Certainly the ball is aged and carries a strange essence. Emotions and happenings linger like a strong aroma and can perfume a dwelling long past its occupants have expired, but this object is of your world and has no unnatural attributes.

"So it's ordinary glass?"

As ordinary as the bed you sit upon. Although I am aware of something else . . . an entity close by, but not clear . . .

"What kind of entity?"

I am unsure . . . There are strong emotions of anger. It's very peculiar . . .

"What do you mean?" I waited for a reply. "Opal, are you still there?"

Silence.

The air around me grew chilly and the ceiling light flickered, then went out. An odd smell filled the room; sweet like vanilla, but so overpowering, I almost choked.

Darkness made me nervous. I had a collection of night-lights and always kept one plugged in. But tonight my walls were murky shadows; the only light flaring was from the witch ball. When I looked down, I was startled to find the glass glowing crimson and blue, like a bleeding sky.

With a shriek, I dropped the ball on the bed. The overhead lights flashed back on and the chilly dampness vanished along with the sickly sweet vanilla odor. I looked down, seeing my own shocked expression reflected in fragmented prisms of glass. And I sensed dark energy from something . . . *someone*.

Nona was right about the witch ball.

It was evil.

3

My hands shook as I placed the glass ball inside a cardboard box. I duct-taped the box, wrapping tape around and around, tighter than an Egyptian mummy. Then I buried the box far back on the closet shelf—like an offering to darkness—and closed the door.

That night I plugged in my angel night-light and lit a white candle for protection. I had no idea

18

what I was protecting myself against, but I felt calm after whispering a prayer and asking Opal to watch over me. I hoped she was listening.

I woke up refreshed; warmed by the sun shining through the window and bursting with ideas for the Booster Club Carnival. Solving problems for a carnival was much easier to deal with than a witchy ball.

On the walk to school, I brainstormed with Penny-Love. She loved my suggestion of a fishing booth, where kids could snag a wrapped gift on a fishing pole, but she vetoed a craft booth. I was into crafts and always working on a new project, like recently I'd finished embroidering a pillow to match my purple-and-white comforter. Creating useful decorations gave me a sense of satisfaction. But Penny-Love pointed out there wasn't time to create and collect craft items.

"Besides, crafts are boring," she said with a roll of her eyes.

I opened my mouth to argue, only Penny-Love's attention switched to some kids walking by and she called out a greeting. Although we'd been friends for a few months, I was amazed all over again by her mega-popularity. Was there anyone at school she didn't know? Doubtful. And she was always being invited to cool parties, too busy to sit around at home doing crafts.

Of course since hooking up with Josh, I'd been busy, too. When Penny-Love and I reached our shared locker, I looked around for Josh. Usually he was waiting for me with a funny story or new magic trick, but today he was a no show.

Of course, Penny-Love noticed his absence, but I pretended like it was no big deal. "His alarm probably didn't go off."

"He needs to get a rooster like you and Nona."

"Except that our rooster is time-challenged. He thinks that 3 AM is morning."

We both laughed and the subject was dropped, although a sense of unease stayed with me. Where *was* Josh? Was he simply running late? Or was he purposely avoiding me? What if someone witnessed my kiss with Dominic and told Josh?

Guilt made me nauseous. When I'd returned from Pine Peaks, I'd considered confessing to Josh—for about two seconds—until I realized he'd never believe the truth. He'd think I was lying if I said I kissed another guy because a ghost possessed me. Josh was a total skeptic, positive anything paranormal was a hoax or could be explained by science. He'd be hurt and think I was in love with Dominic—which was crazy.

Five minutes into first period, Josh showed up. He waved at me, looking a bit embarrassed as he accepted a tardy slip. I was so relieved. Well, not about his tardy. I was glad things were okay with us. Everyone thought we were a great couple, and I was flattered that Josh wanted to go out with me. I loved his high ideals, and being with him made me feel secure. I resolved to never *ever* do anything to risk our relationship.

We had silent reading, then a quiz, which made talking impossible. When the bell rang, Josh came over to tell me he wouldn't be at lunch, but he'd meet me after school by my locker. Before I could ask what was going on, he hurried off to his next class.

Okay, I was curious, but not concerned. Josh had a lot of commitments: student council, volunteer work, and an apprenticeship in a professional magician's society. He couldn't spend all his time with me. I had stuff to do, too, like talk to Manny. So during lunch, I headed for the computer lab.

Manny DeVries, AKA Mystic Manny, was at his usual computer, up front by the door where everyone could see him. His two-finger typing method didn't slow him down as he typed at max speed. His black dreadlocks were tied back in a wild ponytail, and he wore a black T-shirt over safari shorts. Even in cold weather, when everyone else layered on warm clothes, Manny preferred shorts. When I asked him about it once, he said wacky shorts would be his trademark when he became a TV journalist. Then he added with a grin, "Besides, I gotta show off my great legs."

Manny was definitely a show-off. But would he agree to help out at the carnival? I hoped so. As Mystic Manny, he got a kick out of astonishing people with amazing predictions. It was our secret that his unusually accurate information came from me. See, we had this deal. I gave him predictions (harmless stuff like favorite colors and lucky numbers) and he used his investigative skills when I needed information. Like he was helping Nona, Dominic, and I track down this really old remedy book that belonged to my ancestors. So far the arrangement was working out great.

Still, I was nervous about asking Manny about the carnival. I came up behind him, standing there uncertainly while I tried to decide what to say.

After a few minutes, he spun his chair around to face me. "Beany, quit breathing down my neck."

"Don't call me Beany."

"You always say that, but you don't mean it." He flashed the wide grin that made him very popular with girls. I knew him too well to be dazzled by his charm, although I had to admit his dimples were cute. "So what do you want?"

"What makes you think I want something?"

"Don't you?" He arched his pierced brow.

"Well . . . yeah. But not for me."

"It never is."

"I'm trying to be serious here."

"Try harder. Did you know that when you're tense, you get a twitch in your right eye?"

"Do not!" My hand flew to my eye and it felt normal. I noticed he was laughing, and realized he'd been joking. "I don't know why I bother with you. You're impossible!"

"Thanks." He stood and bowed. "Now tell me what you want."

"It's the Booster Club . . ." I went on to explain about the carnival and the idea for a fortune-telling booth.

"Would I get to keep the money I earned?" he asked when I'd finished.

"No."

"How about a fair percentage? Say like 60%?"

"Not even one percent. Notice the word fund-raiser—it means to raise funds for a good cause. Not for a lost cause."

He laughed. "Can't blame a guy for asking."

"So will you do it?" I asked.

"Well . . ." He paused to make me squirm. And damn it, it worked. I thought about how disappointed the cheerleaders would be if he refused. They were counting on me and I couldn't let them down.

"Okay," he finally said. "I'll do it."

I started to jump for joy until he added, "But there's one condition."

"What?"

"So I don't come off like a fake, I'll need some real predictions." He glanced around and lowered his voice. "From you."

My first impulse was to refuse, but then I thought, "Why not?" This wasn't much different from the predictions I supplied each week for his newspaper column.

What would a few more hurt?

*   *   *

Josh was true to his word. After school he was waiting for me by my locker.

But he hadn't come alone, and when I saw the self-satisfied smirk on Evan Marshall's face, I wanted to smack him. Why did Josh have to bring my worst enemy along?

I didn't just dislike Evan. I *loathed* him. He was only out for himself. He used people, never taking the blame for any of his actions. His ex-girlfriend Danielle nearly died because of him. When my helping her resulted in Evan getting kicked out of school sports, he'd threatened to get even with me. Josh may be able to forgive Evan, but I couldn't.

Purposefully turning my back on Evan, I slipped into Josh's arms. I hoped Evan would get the message and get lost.

"I have a surprise for you," Josh told me.

"A new magic trick?" I guessed.

"Nope. You know how I entertain kids as a clown?"

I nodded, thinking of the giggles and smiles when Josh literally clowned around with magic tricks for hospitalized kids. I really loved that side of him.

"Well, Penny-Love cornered me and asked if I'd make balloon animals at the carnival. I figured, why not?"

"Great! It'll be more fun with you there."

"I hoped you'd feel that way."

"Are you coming in your clown costume?"

He groaned. "Do I have to?"

"It's for a good cause. Plus I love a guy in uniform."

"Anything to win your love," he said, his dark eyes flashing.

Love? The word made me uneasy, but flattered, too. I was tempted to ask Josh if he was teasing or serious. But not with Evan's gaze burning into my back. Besides, how could I talk about love with Josh when guilty thoughts of Dominic confused me?

"Evan volunteered to help out, too," Josh said, stepping away from me and patting Evan on the shoulder. "He's in charge of the Hoop Shoot booth. Isn't that cool?"

"Well . . . yeah," I said, swallowing the lie like a big, fat bitter pill.

"I'm glad to pitch in to support the Booster Club," Evan said too smoothly. "Everyone should give back to their school. Don't you agree, Sabine?"

"Uh . . . sure."

"Josh's community spirit must have rubbed off on me, probably cause we've been hanging out since we were kids." He paused. "How long have you been dating—a week?"

"A month," I said sharply.

"Is that all?" Evan flashed a satisfied smirk—like this was a basketball game and I'd fouled while he'd made a perfect shot.

"Evan needed a ride home and since he lives next door, I said I'd take him," Josh added half-apologetically. "You okay with that?"

No way! Evan is an asshole and he makes my skin crawl! He hates me and will do anything to split us up.

That's what I wanted to say anyway. But that would only make me come off like a selfish witch and Evan the nice guy.

"So how about it, Sabine?" Evan leaned toward me. "Mind if I tag along?"

I shrugged. "It's not my car."

"I helped Josh pick out this car, talking the dealer down to a good price, and now Josh is helping me with my studies," Evan added, lightly patting Josh's shoulder. "Once my grades are up, I can get back into sports."

"You've improved a lot already." Josh looked uneasily between Evan and me, probably because he knew I was glad Evan had been kicked off the team. "But maybe we should talk about some—"

"Sabine thinks I'm a jerk," Evan interrupted in an injured tone. "I guess I deserve it, but I'm trying to make it up to everyone. Honest."

You don't know anything about being honest!

"I said some harsh things," he went on, "and I regret it. That's why I picked this out for you, Sabine." He reached into his backpack and pulled out a pale yellow card.

I eyed the card like the plague. I expected to open it and find anthrax or poison. But it was simply a greeting card with a lovely picture of a bouquet of flowers and a simple message, "Can we be friends?"

I'd rather befriend a rabid skunk. I wasn't naive enough to fall for Evan's pathetic gestures. Unfortunately, Josh felt differently, and was staring at me with such a hopeful expression. I couldn't disappoint him.

"Well . . ." I sucked in my pride. "Okay."

But when we reached the car and Josh went around to the trunk to put away our backpacks, Evan grabbed my wrist. "That's not all," he said in a low voice.

I jerked back and rubbed my wrist. "What's your problem?"

"Not *my* problem. Check the envelope." His menacing tone confirmed everything I already thought about him. He was dangerous and still out for revenge.

Making sure Josh wasn't watching, I looked in the envelope.

I pulled out a folded newspaper clipping from the Arcada Hi-Jinx, dated over five months ago. There was a photo of a husky football player, Kip Hurst, waving his helmet in victory. Underneath the photo was the tragic caption: *Star Player Dies in Car Crash.*

I'd had a vision warning of Kip's death, only he refused to listen. I became the school joke—until he died. Suddenly everyone blamed me, as if knowing made me guilty. Classmates, teachers, and even my own mother turned against me. It had been a relief to move away and start over. At Sheridan High, only Manny and our Goth friend Thorn knew about my past. Everyone else thought I was normal, which is how I wanted it to stay.

But now Evan knew my secret.

How long before he told Josh?

4

Horrible dreams chased me into dark corners where there was no escape. A horned devil with Evan's face sprung out. I ran, slamming into walls, stumbling, falling, crying out for help. A light appeared, so bright it hurt my eyes. A shadowy figure carrying a fiery beacon glided forward. Was Josh coming to rescue me? I raced toward it, then stopped when I

31

saw the figure clearly—a headless skeleton! And the fiery ball in his bony fingers was his own skull!

"Sabine . . . Sabine . . ."

"Go away!" I shouted, running but falling again, then finding my back against a solid wall. The skeleton wore Kip's number 17 football jersey. The glowing skull was coming closer . . . closer . . .

"Sabine!"

Jolted awake, I sat up in bed. My heart was pounding and my T-shirt stuck to my sweaty skin. I blinked, trying to sort dreams from reality. I felt exhausted and weak, as if I'd truly been running, and I was a bit surprised to find my room bathed in daylight. Was it morning already?

Someone banged at my door. "You okay, Sabine?"

"Dominic?" I questioned in confusion. He lived in a barn loft apartment and was usually busy every morning with chores. I pulled my covers up and shouted for him to come in.

He opened the door and strode in. "Why are you still in bed?

"I *was* sleeping—until you arrived."

"Don't you know what time it is?"

I glanced over at my bedside clock. "Seven forty-nine. My alarm isn't set to go off till eight."

He shook his head. "It's an hour off."

"No way." I lifted my arm and looked at my silver moon watch. Then I shrieked, "Almost nine! But I'm due to set up at the carnival at nine! I'm late! My clock must be broken. But why didn't Nona wake me up? She was going to drop me off on her way to a client meeting."

"She's still in her room. I didn't want to disturb her—"

"But you didn't hesitate to disturb me?"

"That's different." The corners of his mouth curved, and I tugged my covers up higher around me. He was impossible, helpful one moment and insulting the next.

The house seemed empty without the aroma of Nona's morning tea brewing. She was usually up before me every morning, doing a private ritual of herb tea and gratitude prayers. "I better wake Nona," I said quickly.

Dominic stood there watching me, not making any move to leave.

"Go already," I snapped. "Feed the animals or muck out the barn."

"Already did."

"I have to get dressed, and don't need an audience."

"Too bad. Guess I'll just go."

"Please do."

As he turned, I realized he wasn't wearing his work clothes, but looked especially hot in black jeans, a blue shirt, and a leather jacket. Even his usually unruly wavy sandy brown hair was tamed. "Are you going out?" I asked.

"Yeah."

"To the carnival?" I guessed.

"Maybe later, after my class."

"What class?"

"Shouldn't you hurry and get ready?" Then he turned and left.

It didn't take a vision to know he was avoiding my question. But he didn't owe me an explanation, and I was in a hurry anyway. Thanks to my malfunctioning clock, I'd lost a whole hour. Even weirder—when I looked around the house, I discovered that *all* the clocks in the house were an hour off. What was going on?

I found out soon enough. When I woke up Nona and told her about the clocks, she admitted she'd done it. "It's for daylight-savings time," she said.

"But that's not for another week!" I exclaimed. "And the clocks fall back in October, not spring forward."

Her calm expression changed to confusion, and she buried her face in her hands. "What have I done?"

"Don't worry about it. Anyone can make a mistake."

"But it was more than a mistake."

"It's okay, Nona," I assured, hugging her.

"No, it's not and I'm so sorry . . ." Her words trailed off, then she took a deep breath. "We better get moving. Penny-Love will hit the roof if you're late."

Somehow, I managed to get dressed, grab my supplies, and make it to the community center in record time.

As expected, Penny-Love was frantic when I showed up. I apologized and said it was my fault for sleeping in. Penny-Love knew Nona had health problems, but not how serious they were. Keeping this a secret would be harder as the illness worsened.

Penny-Love assigned me to run the Velcro Toss booth, which meant wearing a bulky sack-like costume with large patches of Velcro sewn all over. Customers would pay a dollar for three Velcro balls, which they would throw at me—a human target. Totally humiliating!

If running late wasn't bad enough, preparations kicked off with disaster. Jill couldn't find the money box, Catelyn broke one of the fishing poles, I forgot to bring the cheesy plastic crystal ball for Manny, and Penny-Love's artistic boyfriend had paints for his face-painting booth, but no brushes.

We were all frantically running around, snapping at each other and complaining that we'd never be ready in time. But gradually all the crises were solved. Jill found the money box, duct tape fixed the broken pole, and Penny-Love made a quick trip to my house for paintbrushes and the crystal ball.

While I was organizing a basket of sticky balls, I heard my name and looked up to find a fuzzy-haired clown with a big red nose and banana-feet flip-flopping toward me.

"Josh!" I smiled at my goofy boyfriend. I loved this playful side of him.

"What kind of costume is that?" he asked, pointing at me.

"An ugly, uncomfortable one." I plucked at the scratchy fabric. "Want to trade?"

"Not a chance. But I have some news that will cheer you up."

"What?"

"You have company." He gestured with his white-gloved hand down the aisle, where a tall, slim girl with masses of long, dark hair was hurrying toward me.

"Amy!" I squealed, jumping over the low booth counter.

"I'll leave you girls alone," Josh said, flip-flopping away on clown feet.

I rushed forward and wrapped my arms around my little sister. "What a great surprise! How did you get here?"

"Mom brought me."

"She did?" I asked, hope rising as I glanced around. "Where is she?"

"Gone. She's taking Ashley to Roseville to visit an old college friend with music industry connections."

"Oh . . ." I tried to hide my disappointment. Would it have killed Mom to come in to see me? I knew she had issues with me being psychic, but we'd gotten along better at my sisters' party. Still it wasn't like she was going to change her attitude toward me overnight.

"I told Mom I'd rather spend the day with you," Amy went on, her blue eyes sparkling under the high ceiling lights. "You mentioned the carnival in your last email and it sounded way more fun than listening to Mom go on and on about Ashley's many talents." She emphasized Ashley's name with a scowl.

"You and Ashley on the outs?" I asked.

Reaching into a basket on the counter, she picked up a Velcro ball and tossed it in her hands. "Do these balls stick to you?"

"Yes. But you didn't answer my question."

She tossed the ball lightly at my costume and it stuck.

"I thought you and Ashley were best friends," I persisted.

"Can we please not talk about *her*?"

I plucked the ball from my costume and set it back in the basket. *Trouble in twin city?* I wondered in surprise. Now that I thought back to the birthday party, Amy had spent most of her time tagging after me. Ashley, on the other hand, was always surrounded by a flock of friends, and carried herself with a sophistication that made her appear much older than ten. At least Amy, who only wore makeup for recitals and modeling, looked her age. But they were both growing up fast . . . maybe too fast.

I didn't press Amy any further, figuring she'd confide in me when she was ready. Instead, I suggested she check out the other booths while I worked. "Get something to eat or have your face painted by Penny-Love's new guy, Jacques. She swears he's the most talented artist in the universe."

"Can't I just stay with you?" she asked softly.

"Of course you can."

So I put Amy to work collecting money and handing out Velcro balls. Right away we were swamped with kids eager to attack a human target. Fortunately the balls were light, so it only tickled when someone scored a hit.

After about an hour of my getting smacked with Velcro balls, Amy offered to take my place. "You deserve a break," she said. "I'll dodge balls for a while and you enjoy the carnival."

"You're the one who should see the booths," I insisted. "I signed up for this, but you came here for fun."

"This is fun." Her dark hair fell across her face. "I like staying here."

I felt guilty for leaving, but I'd been curious how the other booths were doing. So I helped her slip into the ugly costume, then promised to hurry back.

The first booth I went to sold candy and candles, and was run by Nona's friend Velvet, who owned the yummy store *Trick and Treats*. Although she didn't know the details of my grandmother's illness, she knew something was wrong and gave me a special herbal tea for Nona. Before leaving I bought a bag of chocolate caramels and a strawberry-scented candle.

Then I wandered over to the face-painting booth. Penny-Love's new boyfriend Jacques was stocky with alert brown eyes and flame-red streaks in his stubby black ponytail. I watched a moment, studying him. He looked about eighteen, not too macho, but mature in a quiet, intense way.

Next, I watched a skinny boy with bad acne, but a great throwing arm, dunk Principal Cowboy in a tub of water—twice! Then I wandered up and down aisles until I came to Manny's booth. He'd done a great job setting up, with a purple banner waving "Mystic Manny" and glittery decorations of stars and moons.

"Ah, another victim . . . I mean customer." He whisked me behind a dark curtain and plopped me in a chair. He wore gaudy fake jewels and a turban while he sat at a dimly lit table. It was so dark under his blanket-fashioned tent that I could hardly see my own hands. "Are you ready to have your fortune told?"

"Me? You have to be kidding."

"Even doctors must have checkups and teachers need to go to school. It's about time the psychic gets a reading. And I am just the mystic to do it!"

"It's too dark in here," I complained, feeling around for a chair and then sitting across from him.

"Mood lighting. Now sit quietly, my dear, while I consult the crystal ball."

"Usually you just consult me." It had been easy coming up with predictions for him. All I had to do was concentrate on a name and I just *knew* things. Like Lizette's boyfriend had gotten a speeding ticket, Manuel's male cat was actually female and pregnant, and Mr. Blankenship needed to replace his car battery.

"Mystic Manny knows all," he declared.

"Your accent is pathetic. Is it supposed to be German or Russian?"

He held up his palm. "Silence while I summon the spirits."

I shrugged, deciding this could be amusing. Manny would probably say something self-serving like I was destined to work extra hours on the newspaper.

My eyes began to adjust to the dark as Manny waved his hands over the crystal ball and he chanted strange words. The ball flashed like a blazing moon, and I smelled a strong scent of vanilla. A silver-gray aura swirled, making me dizzy.

"You have angered a powerful force," Manny spoke in a raspy voice. "I see much darkness ahead."

So get more candles, I was going to joke, only my throat tightened and I couldn't speak.

"Dire events are churning in motion." He stared deep into the ball, taking his mystic role too far. He even looked like a different person; as if a withered, pale mask floated over his face.

"Nothing earthbound or spirit guided will protect you from the dark journey ahead," he droned ominously. "Destiny is unavoidable."

What destiny? I wanted to shout, but I couldn't even open my mouth. A heavy pressure pushed me down, trapping me spellbound in my chair. *Stop it, Manny! This is all wrong and scary. You're not acting like yourself.*

But his mouth twisted in an angry line and his burning eyes bore into me. "Someone who loves you will cause your death. In five days, you will die."

5

The reddish glow faded from the glass ball and the heavy gray aura lifted.

"What happened?" Manny blinked as if waking from a long sleep. "Sabine, why are you looking at me like that?

I rocked in the chair, wrapping my arms around myself. My head throbbed. I felt both chilled and hot all over.

Manny stood up and drew back the curtain, shining bright light into the tent. "Beany, are you sick?"

Five days, five days . . . the words echoed in my head.

"Say something already. What just happened?"

"Don't you remember?" I whispered hoarsely. "Those things you said . . ."

"I haven't said anything yet." He furrowed his brow. "You only just got here and I was getting ready to read your fortune."

"But you already *did.*"

"No, I didn't. I was going to, but then I . . . well what the hell? That's weird, I usually have a great memory. I don't understand."

"Neither do I." The makeshift fortune-telling tent looked ordinary—until my gaze fell on the table and I gasped. "That crystal ball! Where did you get it?"

"Penny-Love brought it from your house. She said it was sitting on your dresser right where you told her. I was expecting something plastic and cheap, yet this is—"

"The wrong ball!" I finished.

"How could that happen?"

I shook my head, wondering the same thing. I'd duct-taped the witch ball inside a sturdy box and hidden it deep inside my closet. Glass balls can't open doors. So how had it gotten from a duct-taped box in my closet to the carnival? I'd have to talk with Penny-Love, but right now there was a more serious issue.

"You can *not* use this," I snatched the ball from Manny, then found a paper bag and dumped it inside.

"Why not?"

"Because it might be . . ." I lowered my voice so no one could overhear. "Haunted."

"Seriously?" His black eyes widened. "Like with a ghost?"

I nodded, although nothing made sense. If there was a ghost or spirit nearby, why didn't I sense it? It was as if my channel to the other side was blocked. "I have to get this ball out of here before it does anything worse."

"Worse than what?" Manny asked.

In five days, you will die. Of course that prediction was ridiculous. I refused to let it scare me. I was young, healthy, and in no imminent danger. If there was a ghost hanging around, it didn't have the power to do any physical harm. And the witch ball couldn't hurt me either—it was only a chunk of glass.

"I'm taking this back home," I said firmly.

Manny frowned. "Then what will I use as a fortune-telling prop?"

"Pretend to read palms or ask Velvet for some tarot cards. She sells more than candy at her booth, although she might not advertise it. Now I have to go—"

"Not until you tell me why you're so scared." Manny grabbed my arm.

"I'm not scared."

"I don't buy it. Is it that prediction I gave you? What did I say?"

"It's not important."

"Tell me, Sabine."

I didn't want to, but he had a right to know. After I told him, he looked as stunned as if I'd just punched him in the gut. "That's sick. I couldn't possible have said those things."

"You did, but it wasn't really you."

"So who was it? My evil clone?"

"Everything will be okay when the ball is gone."

"Is that supposed to reassure me?" He sank down in a chair and rubbed his hand over his forehead. "As a psychic, I totally suck. Sorry for the rotten prediction."

"It wasn't a real prediction," I assured. "Forget about it."

"That's the problem—I already have. I can't remember the others either."

"Others? What do you mean?" I dug my fingernails into the paper bag. "You gave *other predictions?*"

"Yeah. Although my brain is all foggy like waking up from a dream."

"How many predictions?"

He started to answer, then shook his head in bewilderment. "I-I'm not sure, but before you came there were at least two . . . maybe three."

My heart raced. "Who did you give them to?"

"I don't know." He paused, then gave a grim shake of his head. "I have no idea at all."

6

Amy must have thought I was crazy when I asked her to cover my booth while I left the carnival. I promised to hurry back, then rushed off before she could ask any questions. She was too busy dodging Velcro balls to argue.

I held tightly to the paper bag, afraid the witch ball might escape again. Not that I wanted to keep it! I wish I'd never brought it back from Pine Peaks in the first place. It had been in my distant-cousin Eleanor's attic for decades, and that's where it should have stayed. I could call her and beg her to take it back, but would that stop it from returning?

Nothing made any sense, and I couldn't get that horrible prediction out of my head. I'd told Manny not to worry, that I had no plans to die anytime soon. But I felt a sick sense of unease, and I really wanted to believe my own words. I mean, the idea that someone I loved would kill me was absurd.

Yet I couldn't just ignore it either. It was obvious that a dark entity was spreading evil. I knew confused ghosts could haunt places and buildings, but I never expected to find one connected to an inanimate object. Had it targeted me specifically or was it randomly malicious? At least two other people had received predictions. Had they been told they would die, too?

I longed to ask Opal for advice, only she still wasn't answering. She'd cut off contact with me before, but I didn't think she'd done it on purpose this time. It was as if a wall blocked me from the other side. I had to get rid of the witch ball.

Ducking out a side door, I headed for the parking lot. That's when I realized I had a big problem.

No car—not even a bike. Nona wouldn't return to pick me up for hours.

I was reaching for my cell phone to call her when the sound of a noisy truck engine made me look up. Dominic! His beat-up truck was hard to miss as it pulled into the parking lot. He could be sarcastic and annoying, but he was one of the few people who would understand this situation.

A strong smell of diesel hung in the chilled air as he shut off his engine and stepped out of his truck.

"Am I glad to see you," I told him.

"You are? That's a first," he said with a wry smile. Pocketing his keys, he gestured toward the bag in my arms. "What's in there?"

"Trouble." I lifted the bag.

"A gift for me?" he asked lightly. Then his smile died when he peeked in the bag. "Why are you carrying this around? You were supposed to put it away."

"I did. But it didn't stay."

"What do you mean?"

"Penny-Love mistook it for the crystal ball I bought for Manny's fortune-telling booth and gave it to Manny. Then things got really weird . . ." I paused, not wanting to talk about the prediction

Manny gave me, as if that would make it would real. "Anyway, I was going to take the ball home, only I don't have a ride."

"You do now," he said.

"Thanks. That's half of my problem solved. Now if I could just figure out what to do with this ball."

"I'll take it."

"And do what?" I asked uneasily.

His hands tightened to fists. "Smash it."

A tremor shuddered through me. Was destroying the ball the right thing to do? I wasn't sure, and felt an odd reluctance to give him the ball. I opened the bag, gazing down at dazzling rainbows spun in glass. It would be a crime to destroy such a beautiful antique. I held the bag closer, enjoying a pleasant warmth. I had a mental image of the ball hanging high in a window, shining sunlight into colorful prisms.

When I glanced up, Dominic was watching me with a concern. My emotions lurched. I remembered the kiss we shared—the thrill of his touch, the sweet taste of his lips, and how safe I'd felt in his strong arms. It never should have happened, yet we'd been caught up in powerful feelings that hadn't been our own. Still it felt so real . . . and the memory lingered. I found myself leaning closer to Dominic, lifting my arms and reaching for—

"No!" I jumped back, hot all over.

"No what?" His brows arched with questions.

"No, we shouldn't do anything dumb . . ." I knew I was blushing. "With the ball, I mean."

"So what do you want to do," he hesitated, "with the ball?"

"We need to understand it better."

"If that's what you want."

"I-I don't know what I want." That was the problem, I thought. Everything felt so confusing. And instead of getting rid of the ball, I was hugging the bag like it was a prized treasure. I shoved it at Dominic. "Here. You'd better take it."

"Are you sure?"

No! I thought while I answered, "Yes."

"I know just where to put it for now." Dominic locked it inside a metal container in the back of his truck.

"Is that safe?" I asked, my arms feeling strangely empty.

"Trust me, it's secure." He pointed up at the sky where a large red-brown bird circled, then at

Dominic's whistle, the bird fluttered down to perch on the hood of the truck. He stroked the bird's silky feathers, then ordered, "Dagger. Guard."

I knew Dominic had an uncanny way with wild creatures, still it was freaky to watch him having a conversation with a bird.

"All done," he said. "Let's go."

Then he took my hand and led me back to the carnival.

*   *   *

I was *not* in a carnival mood. I mean, I'd just been told I had less than a week to live—not that I believed that weird prediction—but it was hard to act like everything was fine. Why didn't I let Dominic smash the ball? Was I crazy or something? It was just a chunk of glass. Smashing it seemed the logical thing to do. I still wasn't sure why I stopped Dominic.

To my surprise, Amy and Dominic hit it off, discovering a shared passion for reading. They were discussing J.R.R. Tolkien as they headed for booths. I slipped back into the itchy, ugly costume. At least dodging Velcro balls kept me too busy to dwell on problems. Well, almost too busy. Between hits I worried about Josh, Nona, and the witch ball.

About an hour later, Amy returned to my booth, wearing a balloon hat twisted into the shape of a dog and lugging a large stuffed unicorn in her arms. "Dominic won this for me," she exclaimed. "Isn't it awesome?"

"It's great. So where's Dominic?" I asked.

"Oh he left. Some work he had to do." She giggled. "He takes himself so seriously, but he's really nice."

"You think?" I kept my expression blank, but wondered if his "work" had something to do with the class he'd mentioned taking.

"Oh, yeah. But I like Josh, too," she amended quickly. "He made this hat for me, and asked me to give you a message."

"What?"

"He was leaving early to help a friend study. But he said he'd call you later."

My stomach knotted. "Was the friend named Evan?"

"Yeah, that sounds right. Someone you know?"

"Unfortunately," I said with a grimace. Then to change the subject because my little sister was the Energizer Bunny of curiosity, I turned and pointed to a little girl in ponytails. "Here's another customer."

While I hurried back to the target zone, I thought about Josh. I'd torn up the envelope with the awful clipping and tossed it in the garbage, but that wouldn't stop Evan from telling Josh about my past.

A Velcro ball zoomed toward me, but I dodged to the right.

Evan only dated that girl from my old school to dig up dirt on me—and he'd succeeded. Now he had proof that I was a freak and a liar.

Another ball soared for my head, but I ducked and it missed me.

How could I stop Evan from telling Josh? At my last school, my best friend Brianne turned against me when she found out and even signed a petition to have me expelled. Josh didn't believe in psychics, but he did believe in total honesty. If he found out about my past, he'd hate me for lying.

I forgot to dodge and a ball struck me right in the chest.

When the carnival ended, Amy and I stayed to help clean up by sweeping and packing up boxes. The Booster Club had made over a thousand dollars, which was cause for celebration and everyone was going out for ice cream. But I just wanted to go home.

After the last box was carried out to Penny-Love's station wagon, I telephoned Nona to pick me up. Amy made a call of her own and got permission to spend the night. Amy and I would stay up late watching movies, eating popcorn, and playing card games like we did before I moved out.

It was the best news I'd heard all day.

We were waiting outside for Nona, when I heard someone call my name.

Turning, I saw Manny running toward me. His black dreadlocks flew from his face and he panted from exertion.

"Finally found you!" he said, bending slightly to catch his breath. "I was afraid you'd already left."

"What are you still doing here?"

"Looking for you. Can we talk alone for a minute?"

I glanced cautiously at Amy, who was sitting on the curb absorbed in a thick, green book. "Sure," I said.

Manny took my arm and led me a short distance away. "You'll never guess what I got here. I was packing up my booth and ran across this."

"A notebook?"

"Not just *any* notebook." He flipped it open. "It's the sign-up sheet I put out when I set up my booth. It has some names."

I lowered my voice. "The people who got predictions before me?"

"Exactly." He handed me the notebook. "Check it out."

I looked down and read three names.

7

K. C. Myers
Jack Carney
Jillian Grossmer

I kept my expression calm because I suspected Amy was listening. The first two names meant nothing to me, but it took all my control to hide my surprise at Jill's name.

"Interesting." I gave Manny a look warning him not to say much in front of my sister.

He nodded in understanding. "Thought you'd feel that way."

"Remember anything yet?"

"Nope." His black dreadlocks swayed with the shake of his head. "I doubt I will."

"If you do, let me know."

"Definitely."

The minute he left, Amy put her book away and faced me with a curious expression. "So what was that about? And don't tell me nothing, because I read enough mysteries to know when people are hiding secrets."

I shrugged. "It was nothing."

"I'm not a baby, Sabine. You can tell me anything."

"There's nothing to tell. Just dull carnival business."

"Then show me the notebook."

"No." I held it securely behind my back.

"Why not if it's dull?" She grabbed for the notebook, but I lifted it over my head and spun away from her.

"Oh, there's Nona!" I announced, waving at the car pulling into the parking lot. "Come on Amy."

"You are so not playing fair," she grumbled. But I ignored her and hurried over to Nona's car.

Nona gave a joyful exclamation when she saw Amy, and invited her to sit up in the front seat. Amy hadn't visited since I moved in, so Nona was full of questions about school, modeling, and music lessons. I slid into the back, glad to be alone with my thoughts—and Manny's notebook. Flipping it open, I traced my finger over Jill's flowing cursive signature. Her double L's looped identically and the dot over her "i" was perfectly centered. Super-achiever, even when it came to her penmanship. How would she react to a less-than-perfect prediction?

It would be simple enough to call Jill and find out what Manny told her. But would she tell me over the phone? She'd want to know why I didn't just ask Manny. That would lead to more awkward questions I didn't want to answer.

Besides, Jill hadn't seemed upset today. In the midst of carnival chaos, she maintained a calm, confident attitude. We'd talked several times and she'd never once mentioned a prediction. If Manny had gone into a zombie trance and foretold her death, I would have heard about it—if not from Jill then from someone else. Whatever Manny had told her, it couldn't have been bad news—maybe even good.

Jack and K.C.—whoever they were—probably received good fortunes, too, and I was stressing over nothing. Although, if I was the only one with a bad prediction, that meant the witch ball had a grudge against *me*.

Was it because I was the new owner of the ball?

Or was it more personal . . . *more dangerous*?

When we arrived home, I lugged a folding bed upstairs and set it up in my room for Amy. I was amused to discover her backpack had more books than anything. If it had been Ashley, she would have brought half of her closet plus an arsenal of makeup. How could twins who shared the exact genes be so different?

Of course I shared some of those genes, and look how I turned out. I wasn't fashionable like Mom, multi-talented like my sisters, or a shrewd negotiator like Dad. In a way I was the "black sheep" of the family. I even had the black stripe in my blond hair to prove it; the hereditary mark of a seer. Nona had one, too, until her blond hair turned silver-gray.

While Nona took Amy on a get-reacquainted tour of the farm, I offered to start dinner. I peeled carrots, sliced chicken, and then simmered them with noodles and mushroom soup for a casserole. Savory smells filled the stove-warmed kitchen. Everything was ready when Amy and Nona returned from outside; their cheeks flushed and a piece of hay poking out from Amy's long, dark hair.

Dinner was a festive occasion. Amy and I talked about the carnival, sharing funny stories about the people who came to our booth, like the elderly man who was so excited to score a hit, his dentures fell out. Nona told about her more unusual clients from Soul Mate Matches; the little boy who hired her to find the perfect mate for his father and ended up with his teacher for a stepmother; and the man who discovered his perfect match was his ex-wife. I loved seeing Nona relaxed and acting like her usual self with zero signs of illness.

After dinner, Nona cleared off the table, Amy rinsed dishes, and I put them in the dishwasher. We gathered in the living room and munched buttery popcorn while watching a movie.

Then Nona had work to do in her office, so Amy and I headed upstairs. I was standing in front of my mirror, brushing out my hair, when it hit me that Josh hadn't called. I was afraid to think what this could mean.

"Why are you frowning?" Amy asked, pulling on the baggy T-shirt I'd loaned her.

"Just tired." There were probably a dozen logical reasons why Josh hadn't called; it probably had nothing to do with Evan.

"I've had so much fun today." Amy hugged the stuffed unicorn. "I'm glad Mom let me come here."

"Me, too." I set down my brush and summoned a smile. "Would you like to choose tonight's night-light?"

Her eyes widened. "Really? But you *never* let me touch your collection."

"That was when you were a baby—now you're ten. Go ahead and pick one."

She crossed the room and held her breath almost reverently as she opened the glass cabinet. "The black cat is wicked looking, but the green frog is funny. Oh, I like the musical note, too. Remember who gave you that?"

"Yeah—you." I chuckled. "It was my birthday and you made me follow rhyming clues all over the house until I found the night-light plugged into an attic outlet and tied with a big red bow."

"Wait till you see what I have planned for your next birthday."

I groaned. "I'm scared."

"You should be," she teased, turning back to the cabinet.

A few minutes later, Amy had decided on a stained glass night-light like a Victorian house. "It has a little attic window like the spooky house in one of my favorite books, *The Haunted Attic Mystery*."

"Everything reminds you of a book," I teased.

"I've already read twenty-one this month."

"Wow. I'm impressed."

"Too bad you're the only one." Amy sighed. "Mom says I should be more active and that reading too much will give me squinty eye wrinkles."

"Don't let her get to you. She used to tell me not to wrinkle my forehead and I turned out just fine," I said, lifting my brows in exaggeration so my forehead squished into deep creases.

"You're too funny." Amy giggled. "I wish you never moved out."

"It was tough at first. But it's worked out okay, and it's great being with Nona."

"Not so great for *me*. Mom's always on my case and Dad works so much it's like he moved out. And Ashley . . . well our house isn't a home anymore." Kneeling down, she plugged in the Victorian house night-light. Soft amber, green, and blue lights shone across my walls. But Amy had turned away and stood before my window, staring into the dark night.

Coming up beside her, I slipped my arm around her slim shoulders. "What's going on with you and Ashley?"

"She's driving me crazy."

"How?"

"She's all, 'we're gonna be a famous singing duo.' But I don't want to sing in front of lots of people."

"You're in front of people at your music recitals."

"That's different. I'm not the focus, it's the music. Modeling is okay, too, cause I don't talk much and daydream a lot. It's Ashley who wants to be a diva, not me."

I nodded with understanding. "Then don't do it."

"Ashley already signed us up for voice and more dance classes. She says she needs me because being twins is a good gimmick and will get us noticed."

"Tell her how you feel."

"I've tried only it's like she doesn't hear me. When we were little, I didn't mind letting her decide stuff. But now she tells me what to wear, who to hang out with, and how to fix my hair. I can't stand her."

"You don't mean that—you love Ashley."

"Maybe. But I hate her, too."

The anger in her tone startled me, although I could understand her resentment. It sounded like Ashley was getting out of control—becoming more like Mom. I shuddered at this thought. Two of my mother?

Now *that* was scary.

A short while later, Amy had calmed down and was curled under a blanket with her face half-hidden in a thick, green book.

I was too wound up to relax. So much had happened today, and I hadn't had time to sort through my emotions. I usually chilled out by working on crafts; the repetition of weaving thread was like meditating. But just as I opened my craft bag, the phone rang.

Josh! I thought excitedly. I hoped it was him. Then I'd know we were still okay, that Evan hadn't turned him against me. I might even find the courage to tell Josh about my past.

As I hurried to the phone, I tried to summon a vision of the caller. This was a psychic game I'd played since I was little, and usually I guessed right. But now when I searched my mind for a face or name, I got nothing.

So I had no forewarning when I picked up the phone.

It wasn't Josh.

8

"Good evening, Sabine," my mother greeted in that formal tone reserved for strangers and her eldest daughter.

"Hi, Mom." I paused. "Uh, you must want Amy. I'll go get—"

"No," she interrupted. "I want to speak with *you.*"

"Me?" I twisted the phone cord so it dug into my fingers.

"I apologize for calling so late. But today has been rather hectic."

"Amy said you were staying with an old friend."

"Yes, Trinity VonSchlep, I'm sure you've heard of her work as a casting agent. We were sorority sisters in college and it's been wonderful seeing her after all these years. Trinity is quite taken with Ashley, which could lead to some fabulous opportunities for the twins. But that's not why I'm calling."

I braced myself for criticism. Here comes the *real* reason.

"We haven't had a chance to talk since the birthday party and I wanted to tell you how glad I was to have you there."

"Glad?" This from the same woman who'd told me not to attend the party!

"Sabine dear, you behaved so wonderfully, so poised and mature. I was very proud of you."

Huh? Was I hearing right? My mother—proud of *me*?

"You looked lovely and I was very impressed with your young man," she continued. "Has Josh ever considered modeling? I could put him in contact with some key people if he's interested."

"I don't think so. But I'll tell him."

"Also be sure to tell him he's welcome to visit anytime."

"Should I come, too?"

"Don't make jokes, Sabine. I'm being sincere."

"Well . . . thanks. I'll tell Josh and we'll plan a visit."

"Excellent. He's exactly the sort of young man I'd hoped you'd find, and clearly a very good influence to help you overcome your past problems."

"You don't have to worry about me."

"I'm not—but I'm concerned about Amy."

"Why?" I asked cautiously.

"She's at an impressionable age, and I don't want her to experience anything unnatural. I wouldn't have allowed her to stay with you if I hadn't thought you'd outgrown all the woo-woo nonsense."

Yeah, like I'm going to take Amy to a coven meeting where we'll dance naked with spirits in the moonlight.

Mom hadn't changed at all—my abilities still freaked her out. She'd only called to make sure I didn't corrupt my little sister. Her sugary compliments were as fake as artificial sweetener. Arguing would just bring a quick end to Amy's visit. So I said what Mom wanted to hear—lying through my clenched teeth for Amy's sake.

Then I slammed the phone down.

9

SUNDAY

I woke up early the next morning with a heavy sense of dread, at first not remembering why, then it all rushed back. Manny's ominous prediction, Mom's barbed words, and no call from Josh.

Sitting up in bed, I look toward the window where gray sky was softened by an orange-golden dawn. I refused to let that prediction scare me and

I had lifelong practice ignoring Mom's criticism. But Josh not calling . . . well that worried me.

Had Evan carried out his threat and told Josh everything?

Hugging my pillow, I felt a sharp ache inside. What would I do if Josh dumped me? No more romantic morning meetings at my locker and I'd have to go back to sitting with the cheerleaders at lunch. My friends would be sympathetic, but they'd wonder what I'd done to lose such a great guy. Or maybe they'd know already because Evan would have spread malicious rumors. Then they'd stare at me with suspicion.

Of course, if Manny's prediction came true, I'd be dead in a week anyway.

Stop that negative thinking immediately, a familiar bossy voice said in my head.

"Opal! You're back!" I cried joyfully, tossing aside my pillow and seeing her in my mind. A dramatic vision of tawny skin, ebony hair swept high, and dark brows arched over sparkling, black eyes.

As I've told you repeatedly, I never go away in a physical sense.

"But I tried and tried to contact you, only it was like a wall blocked me."

The obstruction was on your side. I continued to communicate. Your inability to hear me led to a significant amount of frustration.

"It was the witch ball."

The object you speak of is of little consequence, although there did seem to be an unusual aura of discord surrounding it. You were wise to distance yourself from such negative energy.

"Is that why I can hear you again? Because it's not here?"

That seems a likely summation.

"What about Manny's prediction?" Amy stirred across the room, so I lowered my voice. "Why did the witch ball make him say such terrible things? I mean, predicting I have only five days to live. That's crazy, right?"

The course of your future must remain unknown so you can follow your chosen path and learn from experiences.

"So you don't know?"

I am not all knowing, that job belongs to someone else.

"Then the witch ball can't know either."

A logical summation as earthly objects have no insight. But if there is a lost soul involved, what you would call a ghost, I cannot ascertain the scope of its abilities.

"You mean . . ." I clutched my covers to my chest. "The prediction could be true?"

I have no sense of your joining me anytime soon. But there is no certainty when human will is involved and you remain the master of your life chart. When you are ready to come home, rest assured I will guide your journey.

"But when? What's going to happen?" I asked, only I felt her energy draw away. "Opal, tell me!"

Across the room, Amy lifted her head and blinked sleepily at me. "Sabine . . . did you say something?"

If Amy found out I'd been speaking to my spirit guide, Mom would never let her visit again. So I dove under my covers, pretending to be asleep.

When Amy's breathing was even and I was sure she was fast asleep again, I climbed out of bed and changed into jeans and a warm sweatshirt. Tiptoeing out of the room, I shut the door so gently there was no sound. Then I hurried downstairs and out into the chilly morning.

It was so early, not even the livestock stirred as I crossed the driveway and headed for the pasture.

Dominic lived in a loft apartment over the barn. He had a kitchenette and private bathroom, and usually kept to himself. His official job was farm assistant, but the real reason Nona hired him was to locate a long-lost ancestral remedy book. Her episode with the clocks showed that her illness was worsening. I was losing her in small pieces at a time. If we didn't find the book with the only cure, she'd lapse in a coma and I would lose her forever.

When Dominic invited me into his loft, I didn't waste time on small talk.

"Where is it?" I asked with an anxious glance around. With no family pictures on the walls, the loft felt as personal as a hotel room. Yet the way Dominic smiled when he saw me was a warm welcome.

"Locked in the tool shed," Dominic said. I noticed an open window and empty wood perch where Dagger sometimes rested, and suspected the falcon was still on guard duty.

"Thanks for helping out."

"No problem." He pulled out a key from his pocket. "Take this."

"The key to the shed?"

He nodded. "If you want the ball and I'm not around."

I'm the one who might not be around, I thought morbidly as I pocketed the key.

A movement of white caught my attention and I noticed a snowy fur ball curled on top of Dominic's dresser. "Hey, what's my cat doing here?"

"Sleeping."

"So this is where she's been hiding." Lilybelle opened her green eye, then her blue eye. As I ran my fingers across her silky fur, she regarded me for a moment. Then she closed both eyes and resumed sleeping.

"Traitor," I said fondly. "You're supposed to be my cat."

"She still is," Dominic said. "With the witch ball out of the house, she'll return soon."

"Lilybelle doesn't seem to be in any hurry. I think she likes being here."

"What about you?" Dominic spoke with an intensity that made my heart jump. I didn't want to guess what he meant and purposely changed the subject.

"At the carnival, I appreciated you showing Amy around the booths." I cleared my throat. "She loves the unicorn you won for her."

"She's a good kid."

"Yeah . . . she is." He was leaning close to me again. I pulled back, then babbled on, hardly knowing what I was saying. "Amy is shy and wouldn't have left my booth if you hadn't offered to go with her. I would have taken her, but one of us had to stay with the booth. The only other person she knew was Josh, and he was busy, too."

"Yeah. I saw him," Dominic said with a wry twist of his lips. "Nice clown suit."

The way he said "nice" didn't sound very nice at all. More like "stupid and ridiculous." I pursed my lips and said in a cool tone, "Josh is the most generous person I know. Not many guys would give their time for a good cause. He's considerate and wonderful."

"And makes sure everyone knows it."

"That's not true. He cares about people—unlike you."

"I care about *select* people."

"Well Josh isn't selective and tries to make the world a better place. He entertains sick kids in hospitals and at school even the teachers respect him."

Dominic shrugged. "If you say so."

"You don't know anything about him."

"But I know plenty about *you.*" He gave me a deep look. "Can you say the same for Josh?"

"Things have never been better with us," I lied.

"So you haven't told him about . . . ?" He didn't need to finish. Just remembering that stormy kiss made my stomach feel funny.

"No—and I don't plan to."

"Afraid he'll get the wrong idea about us?"

"There is no us." Dominic was so close I could smell his earthy, fresh scent. I stepped away and added firmly, "What happened in Pine Peaks meant nothing."

"Sure about that?"

"Positive. We don't need to feel guilty."

"I don't." He abruptly crossed the room to a mahogany dresser.

While I stood there, not sure what to say or why my face felt so hot, he opened a drawer and withdrew the engraved box that my grandmother had left with him. The box had belonged to my ancestor Agnes and held clues to the location of the lost remedy. When Nona had asked me to search with Dominic, she'd shown me what was inside the box: a family Bible, a photograph of my ancestor Agnes with her four daughters, and two silver charms. Each daughter took a charm when they were split up after Agnes's death. We had two of the charms: a tiny silver cat and a house.

"I found something out," Dominic said, lifting the lid on the box.

"Where the other charms are?" I asked hopefully.

"Not yet. But I showed these to a jeweler."

"Good idea. What'd you learn?"

"They're made of an impure silver that could date back to the Nevada silver strikes."

"Agnes said she was going out west. You think she ended up in Nevada?"

"I plan to find out."

"How?"

"By going there Saturday."

"Were you planning to leave without telling me?" I folded my arms across my chest. "Well forget it. I'm going too."

"Fine with me— but your boyfriend might not like it."

"He won't mind." *Especially if Evan has told him what happened at my last school.* Of course I didn't say that, but thinking it was scary. I liked how my life was and didn't want anything to change.

Dominic was staring at me in that intense way again. Uneasy, I turned from him, saying I had to get back before Amy woke up. Then I hurried out of the loft.

Once in my bedroom, I closed the door behind me. Amy was sleeping with one arm thrown to the side and the other cradling her pillow. Tangled black hair curled around her shoulders and her soft breathing was relaxed. I envied her innocence, knowing my future dreams would be far from peaceful.

I crossed over to my wall calendar by my desk. I picked up a pen and made a note on Saturday: *Nevada/Dominic.*

Looking at the calendar, each dated square of empty white loomed ominously. Moments left of my life. I thought of the deadly witch ball prediction. Five days from yesterday. Placing my finger on today's date, I traced a path across the squares, counting down four more days.

Thursday, I realized with a sick feeling.
Would I make it to Saturday?

10

I had to take control of my future—no matter how short it might be. I was playing a dangerous game where losing could be fatal.

Waiting for calendar days to pass would make me crazy, so I needed to discover what powers I was up against. But I'd already asked Opal, and her answers were less than reassuring. I couldn't ask Nona for advice without risking her health. I considered holding a séance, but Nona had warned me never to invite unknown spirits into our home. So what else could I do?

That's when I had a great idea. Okay, it wasn't that great, but it was the only idea I had, and it was better than sitting around hoping to hear from Josh. I knew he wouldn't call me until after noon since he liked to sleep in late on weekends. Jill, on the other hand, boasted about being an early riser.

I left a note for Amy and Nona, then pulled my bike out of the garage and headed for Jill's house, which was about a mile away.

Jill's stepfather, a scrawny, bearded middle-aged guy named Phil, answered the door in teddy bear boxer shorts and a T-shirt stretched over his belly. "You're too late," he told me. "Jill left for her job already."

Too late? But it wasn't even nine o'clock yet! And what job? Jill was always lecturing the squad that their full-time job was to balance cheerleading and schoolwork. She warned that missed practices or failing grades could get them kicked off the squad.

Phil told me she was at the CVJ Plant, only a few miles away. So I hopped on my bike again. The crisp morning air felt great and I realized I was enjoying myself. Amy and I would have to go biking later. I'd taught my sisters how to ride when they were little and we used to go riding a lot . . . before things changed.

The CVJ Plant was the largest employer in Sheridan Valley. They made pipes and all kinds of industrial materials. Big trucks with the CVJ logo lumbered regularly up and down the roads. But on Sunday morning, the parking lot was almost deserted, only a few cars and semi-trucks. Hulking, darkened buildings appeared locked. I had no idea how to find Jill—until I noticed a side door propped open. Parking my bike under a tree, I approached the door.

"Jill?" I called out, peering inside what appeared to be some sort of delivery entrance. "Anyone here?"

I heard a muffled answer from the back of the building, so I entered and walked down an echoing hall. No sign of Jill, but as I turned a corner I saw a custodian in a brown uniform, pushing a cleaning cart. Wait a minute—the custodian was Jill!

Her blue eyes widened when she saw me, and her hands flew to her face. "Sabine!" she exclaimed. "What are you doing here?"

"Looking for you."

"But how did find me?"

"Your stepfather told me."

"I'll kill him!" She pursed her lips. "No one was supposed to find out where I worked! This is just great—now everyone will know."

"So what?" I didn't get why she was so angry. "There's nothing wrong with having a job."

"Not a job like *this*." She swept her hand toward the cleaning cart. "I can just imagine Penny-Love's reaction when she finds out her squad captain scrubs toilets."

"She won't care," I insisted although I wasn't really sure. Penny-Love had funny ideas about how people should behave and could be very critical.

"I'm so busted." She gave me a pleading look. "Please don't tell anyone."

"I won't say a word."

"Not even to Penny-Love?"

I crisscrossed a gesture over my heart. "Promise. And there's something I want from you."

"Anything."

"Tell me what happened yesterday when you went to Manny's booth."

"Not much." She seemed more relaxed, leaning against the cart. "I only went because Manny is oh-so-fine, like a rebel with a brain. Everyone raves about his predictions and I wanted to see what he'd tell me."

"What did he say?"

"Nothing much. The reading was a total dud."

"Really?" I asked, relieved.

"Yeah. I know he's your friend, but the whole Mystic Manny act is totally fake." She rolled her eyes. "Don't get me wrong, I still think he's cute and he was great to help out with our fundraiser. But his prediction was so far off, it was pathetic."

I let out a relieved breath. "So he didn't say anything . . . weird?"

"Just the usual mumbo jumbo you'd expect from a fake."

"What exactly?"

"Hmmm . . . let me think." She touched her chin. "He pretended to go into a trance and his crystal ball let off this eerie glow. A way cool special effect."

"You have no idea," I murmured.

"The glow got brighter and he kept staring at the ball. Then he spoke my name in a raspy voice and said, 'The person you fear will pay you a surprise visit.'" She chuckled. "You're my only surprise visitor and I'm not afraid."

"Nothing scary about me," I managed to say like I was joking.

"I was hoping for an interesting prediction. Like I'd fall in love with a tall, dark stranger or my mom's lottery numbers would finally win and we'd be rich. But Mystic Manny was a big disappointment."

"How can you be sure the prediction is fake?"

"I'm not afraid of anyone."

"No one at all?" I persisted.

"No. Well, there used to be but—" She stopped, gripping the handle of a broom. "But he doesn't scare me anymore."

"If this guy suddenly showed up, would you be afraid?"

"Can't happen. Impossible."

"How come?"

She met my gaze. "He's dead."

11

The aroma of cleaners and stale air added to the uncomfortable silence that followed Jill's words. I wasn't sure what to say. On one hand it was reassuring to know that one of Manny's predictions couldn't happen. But it was freaky to see Jill so shaken. I'd always admired her calm confidence, yet now she seemed vulnerable.

"I didn't mean to bring up awkward stuff," I told her.

"It's okay." She pushed a stray honey-blond curl from her forehead. "In fact, it feels like I could be real with you and you'd understand my secrets."

"Well . . . thanks. I'm good at keeping secrets."

"You are, aren't you?" She looked at me curiously. "I always thought you were quiet because you were shy."

"It's hard to get a word in with Penny-Love around," I joked.

"Or maybe you don't say much because you have your own secrets."

"Me?" I feigned shock. "Not unless you count the D on my science test that I hid from my grandmother."

"Ooh, big crime. You deserve jail time."

"I confess, I'm guilty." I held out my wrists. "Slap on the handcuffs."

She pushed my hands away, smiling. "You know, it's nice talking to you like this, without everyone else around. Usually I'm all focused on running the squad."

"You're good at it and everyone respects you."

"I got them fooled. You may not know this, but my attitude is one hundred percent bull."

"Nah. Only eighty percent." We both laughed, then she announced that she was due a break. She left her cleaning supplies and led me to a small room with a couch, kitchenette, and coffeemaker.

She poured herself coffee and offered me a cup. I wasn't wild about coffee, so I accepted raspberry tea. We settled on the couch and she turned to me with an embarrassed expression. "You must be wondering why I took such a grubby job."

"Well . . . a little," I admitted.

"I think I can trust you to keep this between us. No one else at school knows."

Sipping my tea, I waited.

"I need this job so I can afford cheerleading. You have no idea how expensive it is—uniforms, cheer camp, and traveling."

"Don't your mother and stepfather help out?"

"My stepfather is husband number four, and he's paying child support for three kids of his own. There's never enough money." Jill sighed. "My mother can't save anything either."

"What about your dad?"

"He's not around."

"Still, he should help with your expenses."

She tensed, looking down at her coffee as she added, "You remember that guy I said I was scared of?"

"The dead guy?"

92

"Yeah . . . well . . ." She met my gaze. "He was my dad."

I was completely speechless and had no idea how to respond. Finally I managed a feeble, "I'm sorry."

"Well, I am, too—but not because he's dead. I caused his death. "

Now I was totally speechless. Mouth-open, jaw-dropping shock. And I had no clue how to respond without coming off judgmental or insensitive.

"You must think I'm a horrible person," she said quietly.

"No . . . of course not."

"Don't be nice. I don't deserve it. I should love my father no matter what . . . but I can't . . . not after what he did . . ." Then suddenly she started telling me more than I think either of us expected.

"Once upon a happy family, or so I thought, I was Daddy's special girl." Her eyes narrowed. "Dad got laid off and was home a lot. He took me to the zoo, on picnics, and to movies. I was so proud to be Daddy's girl, until one night when Mom worked a double shift and I woke up to feel hands touching me . . ."

Her words were raw and powerful, rushing out like a dry river suddenly washed with a storm.

It was like once she started talking, she couldn't stop. Tears flooded her eyes as she told how he said it was because he loved her. He warned her not to tell anyone, but she did. And the police took her father away.

"He died in prison," she finished.

Jill's aura pulsed with purple and red like bruises. Her pain jolted me. I thought of my dad and how he'd taught me to roller blade and play a wicked game of Scrabble. Even though he was busy I received regular emails from him, sometimes a funny lawyer joke or a short message just saying "hi." I couldn't imagine being afraid him.

"So now you know my worst secret," Jill said solemnly.

I pantomimed zipping my lips and throwing away the key.

She pretended to catch the key and tuck it into her pocket. Then she lifted her coffee cup to her lips, made a bitter face, and said it was too cold. Standing abruptly, she crossed to the sink and rinsed the cup out.

I joined her by the sink and washed out my own cup. Neither of us said anything, the noise of running water loud and a lingering scent of coffee.

There was another scent, too, I realized. Smoke? Like tobacco and mint. And when I turned around, a transparent figure loomed over the couch where Jill and I had just been sitting. But this wasn't like my usual visions – the man's face was horrifying; jagged and cloudy, like fragments of a puzzle that didn't fit together.

I heard a gasp behind me and whirled to find Jill staring, too.

"Ohmygod!" she exclaimed. "Dad!"

12

Okay, this was beyond spooky. I was used to seeing ghosts, but not used to other people seeing them with me.

"Daddy?" Jill moaned, shaking and turning white as paper. "But you're . . . this can't be happening! I don't even believe in ghosts!"

Her father regarded her with hollow skull-like eyes. His mouth opened and I thought I heard him say, "Jillian."

She didn't seem to hear him and turned to me with a wild expression. "Sabine, tell me I'm hallucinating. I'm going crazy, right?"

"You're not crazy." I gripped her hand. "I see him, too."

"But he's—he's DEAD!"

"I know," I said with understanding.

"So how can he be here?"

"Maybe he wants to tell you something."

"Or he's mad and wants revenge!" She gave a frightened cry and backed against the wall.

"No, he doesn't." I studied the cloudy figure. Not a ghost bound to earth, but a spirit. I sensed sadness, but also peace and love. His mouth opened and I heard him say, *I'm sorry.*

When I turned to Jill, she was cowered against the wall with her hands covering her face. "Don't let him hurt me!" she sobbed.

"He can't hurt you," I tried to explain.

"Then why is he here?"

"Because he's worried about you and wants to give you a message."

"How d-do you know?" she stammered. "I didn't hear anything."

"Listen, maybe you will. He's calling out to you."

She lifted her head, wiping a tear from her cheek. "Daddy?"

He nodded and spoke her name, but I could tell from Jill's confused expression that she still couldn't hear him.

"He called you Princess," I told her.

"That's what he used to call me." She hugged herself, trembling. "What else is he saying?"

"He's asking for forgiveness."

She ran her hand over her forehead. "I don't know if I can forgive either of us."

"He wants you to know he loves you."

"How can he when everything was my fault?"

He shook his head.

"Yes, it was!" Jill rose to her feet. "If I hadn't told Mom you wouldn't have gone to jail and you'd still be alive."

Again, he shook his head.

"Is he saying something?" Jill asked, grabbing my arm.

"Yes," I replied. "Although it's static-like. He says you did nothing wrong. He was the one who was wrong. And he's very sorry."

"I'm sorry too . . ." Her voice cracked.

"He wants you to be happy."

"How can I be? I messed things up."

"He says if you can't forgive him, at least forgive yourself."

"I'll . . . I'll try." Her eyes shone bright with tears.

"He adds that he won't be able to come back."

Jill nodded, then whispered, "Bye, Daddy."

I thought I saw a faint smile cross her father's cloudy face before he faded to gray. Then he was gone. Only the whiff of mint and cigar smoke lingered.

*　　*　　*

I'd stayed a while with Jill, listening while she talked about her father, not the bad memories, but the good ones. She was still confused, hating her father yet loving him, too. Healing would take time. When we parted, her aura was brighter. And I was relieved she hadn't asked me the tough questions, like why a visit from a spirit didn't scare me and how come I could hear her father when she couldn't.

That was minor compared to a startling realization I had while pedaling home.

Like Manny foretold, Jill had been visited by the person she feared.

The first prediction had come true.

13

I tried not to freak out—and failed.

I wanted to blame this all on coincidence, but what were the chances that Jill's father would appear the day after the prediction? Also, it was hard to ignore the fact that his spirit showed up when I was with Jill—as if I was a conduit for the other side. Would he have still appeared if Jill had been alone?

Like the whirling bicycle spokes, my thoughts spun in circles. Since one prediction came true, did that mean the others would too? I refused to believe I was going to die in five—I mean, four—days. That was just crazy. But what if . . . something *did* happen?

I returned home, both physically and mentally exhausted. I longed to crawl in bed and hide under my covers for the next four days. I'd be safe in my room, and on Friday everything would be okay.

Instead of heading for my room, I joined my sister and grandmother in the kitchen. Sweet aromas swirled around me like a warm hug. Amy and Nona sat at the table, enjoying conversation and blueberry waffles. They smiled up at me, and I thought how much I loved them and they loved me, too. It was impossible to imagine either of them ever doing anything to harm me.

"We saved waffles for you." Amy gestured to a covered plate.

"Thanks." I took the plate.

"You didn't say much in your note," Nona pointed out. "Where have you been?"

"With a friend."

"Well I know it wasn't Josh," Amy said teasingly. "Because he called and asked where you were. I told him I didn't know but that you'd probably be back soon, and I was right."

"Josh called!" I nearly dropped my plate.

"Yes," my grandmother answered. "About twenty minutes ago."

"I'll be right back." I moved for the phone, but Nona stopped me.

"Don't bother, he's not there. He said he'd call when he returned from a fishing trip."

A fishing trip? I didn't even know he liked to fish. But then he didn't know everything about me either—not yet. But I had to tell him soon or Evan would ruin everything.

I didn't say much while Amy and Nona made plans to do something fun before Mom picked Amy up this evening. I didn't care if we went shopping, out to lunch, or saw a movie. My brain was stuck on worry. I didn't believe the prediction, but how could I ignore it? I really needed to talk with someone—and thought of Manny.

Excusing myself, I left the table and went to the phone.

"Hey, Beany," Manny greeted when he got on the line.

I didn't waste any time, and without revealing personal details about Jill, I told Manny his prediction had come true.

"Wow!" he said in awe. "My powers amaze even me."

"It wasn't you," I chided. "It was the witch ball."

"Can't a guy enjoy his moment of glory?"

"Not when my life is at stake. Remember what you predicted for me?"

"Oh . . . the death thing." His tone grew serious. "That's not going to happen."

"Jill didn't believe her prediction either."

"But you're safe. You've got the other side on your side."

"If you mean Opal, she doesn't know anything about the witch ball. And I don't want to wait till Thursday to find out what happens. I've got to take action now."

"Is there anything I can do to help?"

"I was hoping you'd say that."

Then I told him what I wanted.

14

The rest of the day passed quickly—too quickly considering it might be one of my last.

Amy, Nona, and I had a picnic at a River Oaks Park. We goofed around on the playground, swooshing down a curved slide, then kicking high on swings. Nona challenged us to a game of hop-scotch—and won. I felt embarrassed for acting like a kid, but none of my classmates were around, so I figured, why not?

We finished the afternoon by going to *Trick and Treats* for dessert. The owner, Velvet, was delighted to see us and offered us free samples of fudge. We had yummy flavors like cheesecake, caramel pecan, butterscotch, and pumpkin swirl.

Amy teased that she must be in heaven, and I told her she was right.

While my sister examined glass cases full of delicious treats, I found myself studying Velvet. I didn't know her well, but she and my grandmother were close friends and shared an interest in other-world topics. She had no wrinkles, so could be any-where from thirty to fifty. She spoke in a lilting British accent and resembled a proper nanny in high heels, a tailored skirt, and jacket. But in my mind I saw her in flowing robes while she chanted healing spells. There was something almost magical about Velvet.

While Amy and Nona sat on a small wicker table, sipping soda and sampling sweets, I whis-pered to Velvet that I wanted to speak to her pri-vately. She made the pretense of needing my help lifting a box, then we slipped into the back room filled with New Age items like candles, potions, crystals, incense, books, charms, and more. Only select customers knew about this special room.

"Tell me what's on your mind," Velvet said, her brow pinched with concern. "How is your grandmother? Has her condition grown worse?"

"She's doing okay—but I'm not." I hung my head. "Do you know anything about witch balls?"

"Of course." She turned to point at a cluster of delicate glass balls hanging in a display window. "I have several for sale."

"Those are very pretty—but they're new. What do you know about really old ones?"

"Just the superstitions about warding off evil spirits. Why do you ask?"

"Because I sort of inherited an old witch ball—and its ghost."

I explained that the witch ball was a gift from a distant relative who kept it in her attic for decades, how Nona called the ball "evil" and freaked when it moved from my room to the kitchen all by itself.

"And that's not all it did," I added solemnly.

Then I told her about the predictions.

"Oh, my stars!" she exclaimed when I'd finished. "And one of these predictions has already come true?"

"Yes." I shivered. "I was there when it happened."

"So now you're afraid your prediction is real."

"I don't want to believe that, but I can't help being scared."

"Of course you are. This is clearly the work of a disturbed ghost."

"Opal, my spirit guide, said the same thing. But she didn't know anything else, and though I can usually see ghosts, I couldn't see anything around the ball."

"Not a good sign," she said, tapping her fingers against a glass counter. "That means the ghost has unusual powers."

"Like what?" I bit my lip.

"My customers often share peculiar tales, and this reminds me of a haunted, ornate hand mirror in a New Orleans antique shop. No one would buy the mirror because when they looked at it, their reflection distorted into something bloody awful. One lady suffered a heart attack after peering into the mirror."

"How terrible! So what happened to the mirror?"

"The owner of the antique shop decided to destroy it."

"Did it work?" I asked hopefully.

Velvet shook her head. "No. When he tried to break the glass, he felt hands on his throat and blacked out. So he gave up trying to destroy the mirror. He considered calling an exorcist, then had another idea."

"What?"

"He put the mirror and its ghost up on E-bay. Made a bundle and shipped his problem off to someone else."

"Tempting idea." I gave a grim smile. "But I couldn't do that to someone else. Too bad the postal service doesn't ship to the other side."

"More's the pity," she said half-seriously. "It seems to me you have a two-fold problem. You need to prevent the prediction from happening and also get rid of the ghost."

"I can't reason with a ghost I can't see." This haunting was totally different than that ghost I'd encountered in Pine Peaks.

"You'll need to protect yourself." Velvet stared around her room, then strode over to a shelf and picked up a small bottle and handed it to me. "Next time you're near the witch ball, dab on a small amount of this."

I looked at the oblong green bottle with a label that said Chamo-Skull. "What is it?"

"A fragrance used for relaxation."

"To calm the ghost?"

"No—you." She shook her head. "You'll need to be calm so you can perform a cleansing ceremony with holy water and prayers. Be firm when you speak, do not show any fear. Tell the ghost in no uncertain terms to leave you alone."

"Will that keep me safe?" I asked hopefully.

"I can't promise that." Velvet seemed worried, and her high heels click-clicked as she crossed to a cabinet with shelves of bottles, boxes, and potted plants. She pinched off a leaf from a blue-gray plant, sprinkled on a thick dark liquid, then tucked it inside a small satchel, which she fastened with a ribbon around my neck.

"What's this?" I asked, fingering the soft satchel.

"Extra protection . . . just in case." Worry creased in her forehead as she slipped her arm around my shoulder. "Good luck, my dear. You'll need it."

15

Mom showed up promptly at six to pick up Amy. Her meeting with her old friend had gone well, putting her in a good mood. Still, I didn't want to set her off so I wore my satchel under my shirt. I'd show it to Manny at school tomorrow, then deal with the witch ball.

While I was waving good-bye to Mom and Amy from the front porch, the phone rang. Fingers

110

crossed, hopes leaping, I hurried inside and raced to answer. I played my mental guessing game, wanting so badly for it to be Josh that I imagined I saw his face. And I was right.

"How was the fishing trip?" I asked, curling into a cushioned chair, almost giddy with relief that he was still speaking to me.

"I had a great time! Caught this monster fish, only the line snapped and it got away."

"Likely story," I teased.

"Truth! Then I fished for hours with only one little bite that I had to toss back because the fish was too small. But Evan had better luck."

"Evan!" I nearly choked. "He was there?"

"Yeah. Lucky guy caught four huge fish."

Stay calm, Sabine, I warned myself. I took a deep breath and asked, "So Evan went fishing with you?"

"We went out in his dad's boat. Evan's got a real talent for fishing."

And for stringing people along, I thought uneasily. "Did you guys talk about anything . . . interesting?" I asked.

"Sports and stuff."

"What stuff?"

"Nothing much."

I could hear the shrug in his words. If I pushed too hard, he'd wonder why. Still I had to know more. "Did he mention his new girlfriend?"

"If you mean the girl from San Jose, they were just friends. He's thinking of asking Eliza Sampson out."

Figures, I thought in disgust. Once Evan Marshall got what he wanted, he moved on. That's why they called him "Moving on Marsh."

Still, I was relieved Josh didn't know what happened at my old school. Not yet anyway. I'd have to tell him myself—tonight. I wasn't comfortable having him come to my home, so I offered to go to his. But he said his parents had invited friends over, so it wasn't a good time.

"I'll see you tomorrow," he told me.

"No sooner? I really need to talk to you."

"So talk now."

"It's . . . uh . . . complicated." I paused. "I guess it can wait."

"Just till tomorrow. During lunch, we'll sit outside, just you and me."

"I'd like that."

"Oh—the doorbell just rang—the Marshalls must be here."

"The Marshalls?" I bit my lip. "As in Evan's parents?"

"Yeah. They had us over last month, so it's our turn."

"Including Evan?" I sucked in a quick breath.

"He's got to eat, too." Josh chuckled. "Says he has some big news to tell me. Always something going on with him . . . Oh, the doorbell again. My parents must be busy. Gotta go!"

Then he hung up on me.

*   *   *

Josh didn't show up at my locker the next morning.

It probably has nothing to do with Evan, I assured myself. *Josh must be running late. He'll show up soon.*

When Josh was marked absent in our first period class, I told myself he must be sick. Lots of people had colds or the flu. Even our homeroom teacher was out sick and we had a substitute. Still, I worried.

As I walked to my second-period class, I imagined Evan showing Josh the newspaper clipping from Arcadia High, revealing my role in the tragedy. Josh would be skeptical at first, but Evan would repeat what he found out from his last girlfriend.

Everyone at Arcadia High knew the rumors about me and avoided me.

Is that what Josh was doing—avoiding me?

I moved on autopilot, clutching my books to my chest and hunched forward as if my backpack weighed me down. Without meeting anyone's gaze, I maneuvered through the crowded halls. As I turned a corner, I felt a sudden prickling on my neck—a sense of being watched.

Slowing down, I cautiously peeked over my shoulder. Nothing unusual, just the usual mayhem of everyone hurrying to class. But I couldn't shake the being-watched feeling. Goosebumps raised on my arms. Should I hide or walk faster? I chose Plan B, and suddenly sprinted forward.

Footsteps pounded behind me. I thought I heard a shout. Then there was a sharp yank on my backpack and I was stumbling backwards. I cried out and flailed my arms. Someone grabbed my arm and caught me before I fell.

"Who? What?" I exclaimed as I whirled around.

Manny let go of my arm and grinned. "Watch yourself, Beany. Almost had a nasty fall."

"I-I was being chased." I looked around anxiously, still breathing fast. Then I noticed Manny was breathing fast, too. "You!" I accused. "It was you chasing me!"

"I called your name but you didn't stop."

"I never heard you."

"That's cause you were going too fast. Ever consider trying out for the track team?"

"Not even." I readjusted my backpack. "So what's up?"

"I got that information you asked for."

My brain blanked, then a light flashed on. Last time we talked, I'd asked him to look up information on K.C. and Jack.

"What'd you find?" I asked eagerly.

"Not as much as I expected." He handed me a paper. "Check it out."

I looked down at the typed sheet:

K. C. Myers—11th grade, 162 Third Avenue
Apt. 34C
    Emergency contact—Felicia Margo Swann,
    209-555-1925

Jack Carney—12th grade - NFI

"What does NFI mean?" I asked

"No further information—which is odd. All students are required to have contact numbers."

"So what's the deal with Jack?"

"Beats me. Why don't you ask your boyfriend."

"Josh?" My heart jumped. "What's he have to do with this?"

"I got a printout of Jack's schedule and noticed they have the same auto shop class. See if Josh can set up a meeting."

"Uh . . ." I glanced down, the paper shaking in my fingers. "I can't today."

"How come?"

"Josh isn't here."

"So we'll save Jack for later. I'll talk to K.C."

"You have his class schedule, too?"

"Yeah, but there's something odd." He bit his lip. "Apparently he's in my fourth period class—but I've never heard of him."

"He might have switched classes."

"Could be." Manny fell into step with me as I continued down the hall. "If we can't find him at school, we could go visit him at home tonight. You game?"

"Sure. It's a date . . . I mean . . ." I blushed. "Not a date . . . a planned outing together."

"Which describes a date." Manny chuckled. "But we can call it a business appointment."

I nodded, relieved. The last thing I needed was for Josh to hear I was going out with another guy—

even if it was only Manny. Thinking about Josh gave me a sinking sense of dread that stayed with me through my next classes. I even tried calling him on my cell, but no answer.

At lunch, I sat alone in a crowd of my closest friends. I noticed how everyone was paired off except me. Jill with a guy from the student council, Penny-Love hugging onto her artsy beau Jacques, and best friends Kaitlyn and Catelyn were flirting with dark-haired twins named Dan and Derrick.

Everyone asked the same question, "Where's Josh?"

"Absent. Out sick," I explained.

But if he was sick at home, why didn't anyone answer the phone? I tried again and again. If he was too sick to answer the phone, one of his parents would have stayed home with him. Since his brother died from cancer, his parents tended to be overprotective. So someone should have been home.

Not looking good Sabine, I told myself grimly.

And according to Manny's prediction I had only three days left to live. You'd think *that* would be my biggest worry. But no, here I was stressing over Josh. Was that logical?

"Sabine!" Penny-Love's sharp voice snapped me out of my thoughts.

"Huh?"

"Obviously you were zoned out and didn't hear a thing I just said." She gave an irritated flip of her red curls. "Tell Jacques how awful my brothers are. He wants to meet them, but I told him no way. My brothers aren't fit for decent company."

"Well . . . they are kind of rough," I admitted.

"And I have the bruises to show it," Penny-Love said with a groan. "They're like overgrown puppies and think it's funny to throw me around. Total animals!"

Jacques chuckled. "I still want to meet them."

"Not in this lifetime. Last night they played soccer with a pumpkin and smashed it through the living room window. I wasn't even there, but I had to help clean up the mess."

"Tough," Jacques said, dipping a French fry in mustard. "But sounds like you have an interesting family."

"Insane, you mean."

"I still want to meet them. I'm working late tonight, but tomorrow I'll pick you up and you can introduce me. Then we'll go someplace special."

"I'd like that." She leaned against him and they kissed.

Embarrassed and envious, I focused on my plate of some kind of mottled gravy over meat, fries, apple slices, and apple juice. But I didn't much feel like eating. I stood up and grabbed my backpack.

"You leaving already?" Penny-Love asked, turning back to me. "How come?"

"Not very hungry."

"Oh, I get it." She offered a sympathetic look. "You're sad cause Josh is absent, but that's no reason to leave."

"I have to go to the computer lab," I lied. "To help Manny with this week's paper."

"He works you too hard."

"I like hard work."

She eyed me like she didn't quite believe me, then shrugged. "Well, have fun."

"You, too," I replied.

"Oh, I will." She leaned close to Jacques, entwining her fingers through his.

He seemed really into her, too, and they looked cute together. Not long ago Penny-Love had a thing for Dominic, but that never happened— thank goodness. They weren't at all suited. Jacques seemed more her type, kind of edgy but relaxed and friendly. Watching them made me feel sorry for myself.

When I slipped on my backpack, I bumped into the table. Jacques's binder and art history book started to fall, but I caught them. He was so into Penny-Love that he didn't notice. But when I glanced down I noticed something puzzling. There was an inked name on the binder.

Only it wasn't Jacques.

Jack Carney.

16

I'd found Jack!

But what should I do about it? If I asked him about the prediction in front of Penny-Love, she'd want to know why I hadn't just asked Manny. He should remember his own predictions—right?

I stared at Jacques, dying to question him right away. But strategy was required. It wasn't like he was going to disappear, not with Penny-Love hanging onto him like a tight chain. I'd wait until she wasn't around, then talk to him privately—like after school, when he was at his job. I'd find out where he worked and "accidentally" run into him.

So I sucked up major self-control and left the cafeteria.

As usual, Manny was in the computer lab, his fingers clicking across a keyboard. He glanced up, peering through a curtain of dreadlocks, not at all surprised to see me. "I figured you'd show up."

"Why?" I scooted into a chair beside him. "You suddenly turn psychic?"

"I wish. Nah, I just know you'd want to know what went down in fourth period."

"Fourth period? Oh—K.C. Myers!" Memory clicked. He was right—I was curious. "Did you talk to him?"

"He wasn't there."

"So it was a scheduling mistake?"

He shook his head. "Turns out he *is* in my class, but absent a lot."

This made me think of Josh. Not knowing why he hadn't shown up made me worry, especially since I'd heard Evan was absent, too.

"I can't figure out how I can have a class with K.C. and not know him," Manny was saying, gnawing on the end of a pencil. "Am I losing my journalistic edge? Usually I'm observant, but I'm drawing a blank on K.C. My teacher couldn't tell me much except he sits in the back and is quiet, average height, average build."

"An average kid that no one remembers? He has to have some friends."

"You'd think so, but I asked around and nada." Manny made a circle with his thumb and forefinger. "It's like he doesn't exist."

"Well, he must because you found out his address and phone number."

"No one answers at that number. You want to check out the address tonight?"

"Wouldn't miss it."

"Great." Manny glanced down at his leather watch. "Pick you up at seven?"

"Sounds good."

"It's a date.

"Not a date," I corrected in a firm tone. "A business appointment."

Manny threw back his head and laughed.

*   *   *

Since Josh wasn't at school, I walked partway home with Penny-Love. She was floating on a romantic high and had only one topic of conversation: Jacques (AKA Jack Carney). This was fine with me because I wanted to know more about him.

"His carnival booth was really popular," I said casually. "My sister loved the face painting he did for her."

"He's so talented. I keep expecting him to be this temperamental artist, but he's always relaxed and says the sweetest things."

"He seems cool." We waited at an intersection while a truck rumbled by. "I heard he went to Manny's booth. How'd that go?"

"Fabuloso!" She practically skipped down the road. "The best prediction ever."

"Really?"

"Yeah. He didn't want to do it at first, but I dared him. I wanted to go with him, but he made me wait outside the booth where I couldn't hear anything."

I smiled to myself. Penny-Love thrived on being in the middle of the action. Waiting must have driven her crazy. "So how did you find out about the prediction?" I asked.

"Afterwards he told me."

"And?" I paused on the sidewalk to face her.

"He predicted Jacques would fall for a beautiful girl." She stretched out her arms, then pointed to herself. "Me!"

"That's great." But not at all what I expected. Like going to a theater expecting to see a horror movie and finding a Disney cartoon. "You sure that's all Manny predicted?"

"Isn't it enough? It's so cool we both have great guys." With her cheeks blushing nearly as red as her curly hair, she went on about love and dating. I nodded at the appropriate pauses, but my mind drifted. Why had Manny's prediction for Jacques been so different from the ones he gave Jill and me? Was the witch ball messing with us? Or maybe the psycho spirit attached to it liked Jacques better.

After Penny-Love went on to her house, I spent some time with Nona. I felt encouraged as I watched my grandmother bustle around the kitchen, showing no signs of her illness. Vegetable stew simmered in the Crock Pot and warmed the kitchen with delicious aromas.

When I asked Nona if I'd had any phone calls, she shook her head. So I tried Josh's number, only the machine picked up. I'd already left two messages and had too much pride to leave a third. I even checked my email for a message from Josh, but nothing. Skimming through my messages, I found a joke from Dad, two emails from Amy, one from Ashley, and a dozen spams that I instantly deleted.

Unfortunately my problems didn't come with a delete button.

I hopped on my bike and headed for the construction site where Penny-Love said Jacques worked. It wasn't too far, maybe three miles, in a part of town that used to be pasture but was quickly turning into new housing developments.

Right away I spotted Jacques in a group of grubby guys in yellow hard hats, orange T-shirts, and grimy jeans. He wiped sweat off his forehead and raised his eyebrows when he noticed me standing outside the chain link fence.

"Sabine?" he called, slipping a hammer through a loop in his work belt and climbing off a ladder. He met me outside the gate. "Watcha doing here?"

"I was biking and . . ." My mouth went dry; my courage faltered.

Away from school, Jacques seemed older, rougher, and the narrow glint in his eyes bothered me. His tough-looking co-workers didn't reassure me, either. I recognized one of them from school; he was rumored to be involved in dealing drugs. Of course, rumors weren't always true.

Jacques shifted on the oil-stained pavement as he faced me. "You okay?"

"Yeah." I swallowed. "I wanted to ask you something, but if you're busy . . ."

"Work can wait." He gave me a wink. "This something you'd rather Pen didn't hear?"

"Well . . . I guess."

"You looking for some action?"

I gave him a blank stare, my pulse jumping. I wasn't sure if he meant drugs or sex, and didn't want to find out.

"No," I said coolly. "Definitely not."

"Hey, I was just messing with you. I know you're cool." He patted my shoulder as if to reassure me—but it did the exact opposite. "So what'd ya want to ask?"

"About the prediction you had at the carnival."

"Oh that. I don't go in for that mystic stuff, but Pen insisted, so I figured what the hell?" He shrugged like he didn't take anything seriously, expecting life to be an easy ride where other people did the driving.

"Did anything strange happen when you talked to Manny?"

"Nothing, but that dude was totally stoned or something."

You would make that assumption, I thought. I found myself liking him less and less. But I kept my opinions to myself. "Did the crystal ball seem . . . odd?"

"Yeah. There weren't any electric cords yet it blazed like it was on fire. It even floated off the table. Way cool! How'd he do that?"

"Trick lighting."

"Well, it blew me away. Best part of the show."

"What'd you think of your prediction?"

"Not much. " He spat into a pool of oil on the pavement. "Total bull."

"But I thought you liked it. Penny-Love raved about how great it was."

"That's cause I told her what she wanted to hear. Got to keep my girl happy," he said with another one of those smarmy winks. "She's a pushover for romantic crap."

"So Manny didn't say you'd fall for a beautiful girl?"

"Nah. I made that up."

He grinned—then told me the real prediction.

17

"You're supposed to fall off a horse?" I asked in amazement. It wasn't as sappy as falling for a beautiful girl, but definitely *not* what I expected. "Are you sure you heard him right?"

"I wasn't hung over or anything if that's what you were thinking."

"That's not what I meant." My hair fell across my face as I glanced over at the construction site.

Falling off a roof or ladder would make sense, but a horse? This was an area zoned for new housing developments, not livestock. And Penny-Love told me Jacques lived in an apartment near Main Street.

"I know what I heard," Jacques said defensively. "That mystic dude said all hollow-like, 'You will suffer a severe injury from a fall off a horse.' But no way that's gonna happen."

"How can you be sure?"

"I'm allergic to horses. When I was a kid, I had to be rushed to the emergency room after riding a pony. Man, I almost died. After that I wouldn't even go near merry-go-round horses."

"You don't ride at all?"

"Never. I can't look at a horse without sneezing. I steer clear of the beasts."

"That's great," I said, then noticed his look of surprise, and added that I meant it was great he wouldn't have a dangerous fall. But I was actually thinking it was great that his allergy prevented the prediction from coming true. If his prediction couldn't happen, the witch ball ghost had no real power. My prediction wasn't going to happen either.

Jacques glanced over his shoulder to where a semitruck pulled into the site. "That all you need?"

"Yeah."

"I better get back to work," he said with a wave.

I waved back, then hurried to my bike—eager to get away from him. His information may have been good news for me, but his whole sleazy attitude was bad news for Penny-Love. She thought Jacques was mellow because he was a creative artist. But I suspected it had more to do with drugs. When she found out, she was going to be devastated.

Should I tell her? And if I did, would she believe me?

*   *   *

Penny-Love wasn't the only one with a troubled romance.

When I returned home, I found out that Josh *still* hadn't called—and I blamed it on Evan. He must have carried out his threat and told Josh all about me.

Disappointment shifted into anger. I mean, so what if I'd kept a few secrets from Josh? There were things he hadn't told me either, like all those meetings he had with his magician society. I respected his privacy, so he should respect mine. But the fact that he hadn't returned my calls proved otherwise.

Well, fine! I didn't need someone around who was so quick to judge me. If he couldn't deal with my past, then I'd have to deal with losing him. Still, if the roles were reversed, I would have told me in person. Avoiding me was cowardly; not what I'd expect from Josh.

I was staring at the phone, dreading and hoping it would ring, when I heard gravel crunching. Glancing out the window, I saw a car coming down our driveway. My heart leaped and I hoped it was Josh. But no such miracle.

Instead it was Manny, and he'd brought a surprise—Thorn.

When Manny introduced me to Thorn, it had been mutual suspicions at first sight. She had a personality as prickly as her nickname. Her multiple piercings, exaggerated makeup, and morbid black outfits screamed rebel, while I was into casual, brand-name styles. But Manny pushed us together, and we'd become friends. Not that this went over well with my other friends, especially Penny-Love who had a low opinion of Goths.

I'd gotten closer to Thorn on the trip to Pine Peaks, learning her real name (Beth), her true hair color (dark blond), and her mother's profession (minister).

Today she wore black leather pants, a black jacket, a spiked collar, and a belt woven with barbed wire. But instead of her black shoes, she wore bright pink sneakers that matched the pink rhinestone pierced through her eyebrow.

"Pink is the new black," Thorn said when she caught me staring. "I'm thinking of getting a pink-and-black wig."

"Go for it." I grinned.

"Manny filled me in on the weird predictions and I couldn't resist coming along. I hope it's okay."

"It's better than okay," I told her honestly. She was the first person my age I'd met with a psychic ability, although she downplayed her skill for finding things as just a game. It had been more than a game when she helped find a classmate who was bleeding to death. Her game had helped save a life.

"I figure I can help you guys," Thorn said as she buckled up in the front seat.

"Because you're a Finder?" Manny teased, knowing Thorn hated labels, especially on her.

"Not even." She shot him a scathing look. "I can help cause I have a friend who lives in the same apartment building."

I pulled against my seatbelt, leaning forward from the backseat to face Thorn. "Does your friend know K.C.?"

"No. She says I must have the wrong apartment number, because only a woman and a girl live there."

A thought hit me I hadn't considered before. "Could K.C. be a girl?"

Manny shook his head. "Not according to the school records."

"Maybe he moved and didn't tell the school," Thorn suggested.

"Easy enough to check out. There's something weird about a dude no one knows."

"Nothing wrong with being independent, not a follower," Thorn said with a critical glance at me.

"He could be shy," I said a bit defensively.

"Or invisible," Manny joked. He clicked the right-hand signal, then drove down a street with few lights and fewer street signs.

Not the best part of town, I thought uneasily as I noticed seedy figures milling around corners. Thorn directed Manny to a shabby three-story apartment complex. Even in the dim light, it was clear it needed a paint job and new roof. We found stairs and walked up to the third floor.

"You girls wait here," Manny said as we neared apartment 34C. "I'll go ahead to check things out."

"And have all the fun without us?" Thorn retorted. "I don't think so."

"It's safer for only one of us to go ahead."

"So why should it be you? Because you're a guy?" Thorn arched her pink-studded brow. "FYI— I've taken self-defense and kick-boxing lessons. You, on the other hand, freak out over a paper cut."

"Just that one time," Manny insisted. "My thumb was bleeding."

"Wimp."

"Well you're a heartless—"

"Enough." I stepped between them. "This is my problem, so I'll go ahead."

Before they could stop me, I pushed past them to knock on the door. Glancing behind me, I put my fingers to my lips, gesturing for them to stay back.

When I heard footsteps behind the door, I forced a calm expression. A lifetime of pretending not to see ghosts or hear spirits made it easy to mask my emotions. Only my pounding heart betrayed my anxiety. What was I doing here anyway? If K.C. answered the door, what should I say to him? I couldn't just blurt out, "Had any death pre-dictions lately?"

So I was kind of relieved when a middle-aged woman answered the door. She had tired lines etched in her skin and her black hair was tied back in a scarf. She gave me a dismissive look. Her hand clutched the knob, poised to slam the door in my face.

"I'm not buying anything," she said briskly.

"Good, because I'm not selling."

"Then what do you want?"

Deep breath. "I'm looking for K.C."

"Why?" she demanded. "What do you want with him?"

"We, uh, go to school together. Does he live here?"

"Of course he does, I never said he didn't. I'm responsible for him after all."

"Are you his mother?"

"Do I look old enough to have a teenager?" She glared at me, and I was glad she didn't wait for an answer. "His mother is my oldest sister, only she went and got her butt thrown in jail, so I took in K.C. and his sister."

"That was kind of you." I tried to look behind her, hoping for a glimpse of K.C., but saw no movement except the flash of a TV. "May I speak to K.C.?"

"No, 'cause he's not here. He's out with friends."

"What friends?" I asked, surprised.

"Who can keep up?" She shrugged. "He's so popular, always rushing off to parties and school activities."

Popular? Parties? Were we talking about the same person?

"Do you know his friends addresses or phone numbers?" I asked. "It's really important I talk to him."

"About what?" She eyed me suspiciously.

"Uh . . . a school project. When do you expect him back?"

"I'm not his secretary. And I got enough to deal with my niece, so if you don't mind, I have to get back to—"

"Wait!" I stuck my foot in the doorway. "Could I talk with your niece? Maybe she knows—"

"Zoey's only five and doesn't know anything. Don't bother me anymore."

Then she kicked my foot aside and slammed the door in my face.

"I feel sorry for Zoey," Thorn said, coming up beside me. "That woman is a walking bad attitude."

"I didn't handle that very well," I said with an apologetic shrug. "I should have let you guys talk."

"You were fine," Manny assured.

"Except for calling her old and getting the door slammed in my face." I sighed. "Now how do we find K.C.?"

Manny turned to Thorn. "Do your 'finder' thing."

"Not so easy. I'd have to hold something that belongs to him. It's not likely that woman will give us anything."

"I picked up this weird vibe from her, like she was afraid of something or someone." It was hard to explain the uneasy feeling that nagged at me. It came with colors of grays and reds—but no clear answers.

"So who's she afraid of?" Thorn said. "What if K.C. is the violent type?"

"We better find out." Manny rubbed his chin and stared thoughtfully at the closed apartment door. "Let's go talk to some neighbors."

No one answered in the first two apartments we tried, although I sensed movement beyond the peepholes. I guess people around here were naturally suspicious. An elderly man who was hard of hearing, which made questioning him impossible, opened the third door. At least someone answered at our fourth try—a dude with a shaved head who had wrestling blaring on his TV. But when we asked about K.C., he said he'd never heard of the guy.

Thorn suggested we talk to her friend, then led us downstairs. Her friend, Kevin, was a skinny black-draped guy with white makeup and enough piercings to set off every metal detector within a mile. He confirmed only the woman and her niece lived in 34C.

When we finally left the apartment complex, even I was beginning to doubt K.C.'s existence. Maybe Manny was right—the guy was invisible.

By the time I returned home, I was confused, exhausted, and discouraged.

But my mood improved when I found out I'd had a phone call.

From Josh.

18

"What did he say?" I almost pounced on my grandmother.

"I wrote it down so I wouldn't forget. Now where did I put that paper?"

We spent twenty minutes searching for the note, until finally I spotted it propped on the side of the refrigerator with a magnet.

Nona pushed back her gray-blond curls, her cheeks flushed apologetically. "I don't remember putting it there."

I told her it didn't matter, but we both knew it did. More evidence that her memory was diminishing. I was losing her by inches.

Looking down at the pink paper in my hand, I read Josh's message.

Locker tomorrow. Love Josh

"That's all?" I asked, flipping the note over and hoping for more, like where he'd been all day and why he hadn't called sooner.

But at least he *had* called and he wanted to see me in the morning. So I guessed our relationship was okay. It was amazing how much lighter I felt; like my feet soared off the ground and I floated near the ceiling. If Evan had tried to poison Josh against me, it had failed. Josh still cared enough to end his message with "Love Josh."

Under the glow of a heart-shaped night-light, I fell asleep smiling.

Getting ready for school the next morning took extra time. I tried on a dozen outfits, hated them all, and finally settled on jeans and a yellow T-shirt. Then I spent at least thirty minutes fixing my hair, choosing the perfect pair of earrings, and applying makeup. When I ran into Penny-Love when I reached school the next morning, she said I looked hot.

Ironically, now that my boyfriend was back at school, hers was gone. Jacques (AKA Jack) hadn't called last night or kept a promise about driving her to school. In her usual dramatic jump of conclusions, she was sure this meant he'd found another girl.

"I knew it was too good to last," she said, stepping away from the crowds of kids entering the building. "Guys always disappoint me, why should Jacques be any different? I was going to enroll in an art class, so we'd have more in common. He's older and smarter, why would he want to be with me?"

"Because you're smart, gorgeous, and fun. You're the one who's too good for him. Lots of guys would love a chance with you."

"I've gone out with a ton of guys and they don't compare to Jacques. But your loyalty is sweet," Penny-Love said with a sad smile.

"I just want you to be happy."

"I will be when I find out Jacques has a good reason for being absent—like a severe illness."

"Mono? The kissing disease?"

"Not that severe!" She realized I was teasing, then we both laughed.

We headed in different directions and minutes later I found Josh waiting by my locker. He grinned when he saw me and I could tell he liked how I looked.

"Sabine," was all he said and then his arms were around me and we kissed right there in the school hall. Usually Josh was ultrareserved, but I didn't mind this change.

"So where were you yesterday?" I tried to sound casual as I spun my locker combination and pulled out my English book.

"With Evan."

"Evan!" My grip on my book tightened.

"Yeah. You know we went fishing Sunday."

I nodded, unease mounting.

"Well he left his backpack on his dad's boat, and he needed it for his Biology class. But he had no way to get out to the boat. His parents had already left for work and he doesn't have his own car."

"So Josh to the rescue?" I tried not to sound sarcastic, and failed.

"Hey, what else could I do?" He spread out his hands. "If he flunks this makeup test, he won't get back on the team. Besides, I figured we'd be back before school started. But it didn't work out that way."

"So what *did* happen?"

The warning bell rang and we walked down the hall. Josh quickly filled me in on the rest of his story. It was unbelievable, but coming from Josh, I knew it must be the truth.

Josh had driven Evan to the marina where the boat was docked, got on the boat, and found the textbook. But the ropes mooring the boat came loose and they drifted away from the dock, out into the middle of an icy mountain lake. Evan didn't have the ignition keys to the boat (why did this *not* surprise me?). They couldn't swim back because the water was too cold. Evan had a cell phone, but couldn't get a signal. So they waited all afternoon for another boat to show up and tow them in.

"By then, school was out and so were you," Josh finished. "Where'd you go?"

I hesitated. "After a newspaper interview."

"When'd you start doing interviews? You're a copy editor."

"Yeah, but Manny was shorthanded."

"You shouldn't let that guy bulldoze you into doing his work. I don't like how he's always taking advantage of you."

"Like Evan does with you?"

"Message received." Josh gave a rueful smile. "I know you're right, it's just hard to refuse Evan. When my brother was alive, he and Evan were my heroes and I was the pesky kid tagging along. Now it's only me and Evan . . ."

He paused, staring into space. The subject of his brother was private and rarely brought up. When he'd first told me about his loss, I'd wondered if his brother would try to send him a message through me. But there hadn't been anything, and I doubted Josh would be open to hearing a message anyway.

I purposefully switched topics. "That was a long time to be stuck on a boat. What'd you and Evan do to keep busy?"

"Fished. Studied. Talked."

"Talked about what?" I tensed. "Did Evan say anything about . . . about me?"

"Nope. Why should he?"

"No reason. But when girls get together, we talk about guys."

"You talk about me when I'm not around?"

"Tons. And it's all good," I linked my fingers through his as we neared our homeroom.

"So what about that interview?" Josh asked. "How did it go?"

"Not so good," I admitted, reliving the slam of the door in my face.

"It'll work out next time. I have faith in you."

Looking into his handsome face, I wondered if he'd still feel that way when he learned I'd been kicked out of my old school and labeled a freak. I wished I could avoid telling him forever, but if I didn't tell him, Evan would.

In first period, I tuned out my teacher and wondered how to explain my psychic ability to Josh. We'd already had a discussion about magic and he'd made it clear he was a skeptic. He believed magic was an illusion created solely for entertainment. How could I convince him ghosts existed and that my psychic visions foretold the future?

I was still thinking about it during break when I heard someone call my name. Glancing down the hall, I saw Penny-Love running toward me. She clutched a cell phone in one hand and ran her fingers through her wild curls with the other.

"Oh, Sabine! I just found out why Jacques is absent."

"Why?" I asked, immediately concerned by her flushed face and reddened eyes.

"There was an accident last night! He was in the hospital."

"An accident?" I inhaled sharply. "What kind?"

"He fell on the job and fractured his arm."

"That's terrible!"

"Even worse—it was his right arm, so he won't be able to paint for weeks. He slipped because he had oil on his shoes and didn't realize it. Poor Jacques."

"Oil?" I thought of the oily puddles on the pavement where we talked last night. Is that how the oil got on his shoes? Was I somehow responsible?

"He fell off a board."

"A board? Why not just use a ladder?"

"Not a regular board—it was stretched out like a plank and propped up on the sides. He had a name for it." She paused, her reddish brow knit in concentration.

My heart skipped. "What?"

"A sawhorse."

19

A horse—a freaking sawhorse! It was all so weird! Jill's visit from her dead father and now Jacques falling from a horse.

During sixth period, I couldn't concentrate on editing and must have fixed the same misplaced comma a dozen times. I kept glancing across computer consoles to a large wall calendar where dates marked my fate.

Two days to live?

I was trying so hard not to believe the prediction could happen, as if believing would make it a reality? My world had been flipped upside down and everything was out of control. This was *not* how my gift was supposed to work. I'd always been the one who gave predictions. I wasn't supposed to *receive* them.

I couldn't pretend the witch ball was harmless anymore—not after two predictions came true. Dangerous powers were at work, and if I didn't figure out how to stop them, I could end up dead.

If only I'd never taken the witch ball. *I should have sent it back up to the attic,* I thought as I stared down at blurry papers. Why didn't Opal warn me?

Would you have listened if I had?

I clearly heard her voice as if she were standing beside me.

She had a valid point. Would I have listened to her? Probably not. I was quick to give advice for other people, but reluctant to take it.

"But I'm ready to listen now," I thought to her. "What should I do?"

Face your fear.

"How do I do that?" I asked, then reddened with embarrassment when I caught a boy sitting in the seat next to me giving me a curious look. Oops! Guess I must have spoken aloud.

Pressing my lips tightly shut, I picked up the article I'd been proofing, and pretended to work. Out of the corner of my eye, I saw the boy shrug and turn away.

The connection to Opal was gone, so I replayed her advice in my head. *Face your fear.* Not "fears" but "fear," as in a specific fear. There was only one fear I could think of—the witch ball.

I'd had some experience with ghosts, who were usually earthbound because they were confused and too frightened to move on. I had mixed feelings about dealing with ghosts, although it always felt good when I helped a lost soul find peace.

But the ghost around the witch ball was elusive—and frightening. If I confronted it, more trouble could be unleashed. The ghost had already shown uncanny abilities, moving the ball from my closet to Nona's kitchen and switching places with the crystal ball meant for Manny. I didn't want to mess with a ghost with that sort of power.

But doing nothing wouldn't accomplish anything either.

So I had to confront my fear like Opal said.

I hoped I wouldn't regret it.

*　　*　　*

After school, I dropped off my backpack in my bedroom, checked in on Nona who was talking on her office phone, then went outside. I headed for the shed behind the barn. I spotted Dominic working in the back pasture, and had a strong urge to ask him to come with me. But if I told him what I planned to do, he might try to stop me. I had to do this alone.

I clutched the key Dominic had given me, the metal cold against my skin. I felt cold, too. The sky had grown overcast and a chilly wind shivered through my jacket. I wrapped my arms around myself, wondering if I should go back for a heavy coat. I might need an umbrella, too, in case it started to rain.

Procrastination only moves you backwards, a haughty voice rang in my head.

"Opal, I'm so glad you're here."

I know nothing about this earthbound soul you seek and find myself in the unusual situation of uncertainty.

"That doesn't exactly reassure me."

Reassurance is not my purpose. Also, you will not require an umbrella, the precipitation will hold off until this evening.

The toolshed was out behind the barn, half-hidden in a grove of oaks. It was a ten-by-ten wooden structure, the roof sagged in one corner, and the paint was faded with age. As I reached to unhinge the latch, my hand shook. I thought of a dozen reasons why I should turn around and forget this whole idea. But I'd come this far and didn't want to give up now.

As I began pulling the door open, I heard flapping wings. I looked up to see Dominic's falcon. Dagger swooped down low, squawking as if he was admonishing me. His wings brushed my arm, but I ignored him and finished opening the door.

A dark, musty smell swirled around me as I entered the shed. Something gauzy flew across my face and I shrieked. Jumping back, I saw fragments of a cobweb clinging to my fingers. I slapped it away, swallowed hard, and stepped deeper into darkness.

I had to blink a few times before my eyes adjusted and I could recognize the distorted shadows as gardening tools; a rake, broom, and hoe were propped against the wall in one corner. There were also old crates, a rusted push mower, and bags of fertilizer. That would explain the ripe odor.

A sudden gust of wind roared and shook the building, nearly knocking me over.

The door banged shut.

I grabbed onto a shelf to pull myself up, then tried the door. I pushed at the rough wood, but it wouldn't budge. Panic closed in around me like a straight jacket and I felt trapped. Coming here had been a bad idea. I wanted out now—even if it meant breaking down the door.

Looking around desperately, I started to grab a shovel. But I stopped in mid-reach when I noticed a silvery glint off a large square box. The metal chest. My gaze zeroed in on the heavy metal lock and I lifted the key from my pocket. A perfect fit into the lock. There was a loud click and the lock fell open.

My hands grew clammy and the urge to flee was stronger than ever. I could sense Opal with me, but no other presence. To be safe, I reached up under my collar and touched the protective satchel

Velvet had given me. It as soft, warm, and comforting. I just hoped it had real powers to ward off evil.

As I lifted the lid of the chest, an unearthly golden glow lit up the darkened room, like a curtain drawing back from the moon. My breath caught as I stared down at the beautiful crystal globe. Inside, tiny glass shards blazed with dazzling rainbow colors. These colors danced across the walls, and I felt as if I moved with them. My fears faded, replaced with the most wonderful sensation—warm, joyful, pure happiness. Without thinking, I reached for the witch ball—

No! Opal's voice rang out sternly. *Don't touch it!*

I lurched back, blinking in confusion. The wonderful feeling died and lovely rainbows eclipsed to black. I was left with a sharp disappointment.

Sabine, do not lower your guard. She is close and watching.

"She?" I looked around. "I don't see anyone."

BANG! The lid on the steel chest clanged shut.

The witch ball ghost! Like a genie released from a lamp, she was here with me. Yet I still saw nothing.

"Where is she?" I cried, circling slowly in place on the alert for the slightest movement.

Close your eyes and concentrate on her image.

I did as asked, but I only saw Opal—her black upswept hair, heavy, dark brows over intense, black eyes. She floated several feet off the ground and seemed to be watching the steel chest. No witchy ghost.

So I opened my eyes—then gasped. The witch ball was rising into the air. I knew there had to be a ghost guiding the ball, but I still couldn't see anyone, not even an aura.

She's blocking you. Concentrate to a meditative state.

I would have rather smashed open the door and fled from the shed.

Instead I sat on a crate and closed my eyes tightly. Nona had taught me how to meditate when I was little, explaining that I needed to visualize a place where I go and feel safe. So I shut out all fears and hummed softly, becoming at one with my rapid heartbeat and closing off everything but my thoughts.

I imagined a peaceful island with a beautiful white gazebo where windows faced the ocean in every direction. I heard the soft lapping of ocean waves and smelled a garden of fragrant flowers surrounding me with comfort. I was no longer in a manure rank shed, but secure in my own paradise.

Watching through a window in this perfect place was like peering outside a fragile glass dome. And for the first time I saw *her.*

Two figures faced each other. Opal and a pale woman, tall and bird-like, with narrowed no-color eyes and a bitter scowl. Her hair was braided in a bun; an old-fashioned style that matched her long drab skirt that dragged behind her like a dark veil. She wore a high-necked blouse of heavy brown fabric with long sleeves and tiny pearl buttons. She was all dark energy except for the globe of rainbow light she clutched protectively in her arms. The witch ball.

I wanted to ask who she was, but in my peaceful sanctuary, I was only a spectator.

Opal swept towards the woman, her chin lifted high with confidence. *I am Opalina Christine Consuela LaCruz, and might I know your name?*

"Hortense." The woman held tightly to the witch ball and regarded Opal with suspicion. "I know what you want, and all the others before you."

I want nothing from you, instead I can offer you assistance to a better place. Allow me to guide you to—

"Nay! I will not be fooled. My ball is mine alone and no one will wrench it from me. Be gone or harm will befall you."

What harm can you do from your dark prison? I am free to go between worlds, while you are trapped in a hell of your own making. Freedom is yours if you go forward with me and find joy away from this chosen exile.

"You seek to lure me away from my ball."

Earthly possessions have no lasting value.

"Lies! I watched them come, peeking into my home and calling for me to come out, but I would not be fooled. They were tools of the devil and conjured magic against me, only no harm would befall me as long as my witch ball offered protection."

You need no protection if you go into the light. Come with me—

"Your feeble attempt at trickery will not work. I recognize you for your sins when you lived on earth."

My past was a trial on a path leading to wisdom. That was hundreds of earth years ago and has no relevance. I do not fathom how you even know these things.

"I know that and much more. Leave before I show the full force of my powers."

Let go of your anger and trust me—

"Trust a woman who took her own life, leaving her children alone? I would have given my life for my child, yet even that was denied me. I will not place my trust in someone such as you," she sneered. "Begone!"

Turbulent seas rose up around my glassed-in house, then swept me back to reality. My eyes opened and I gasped, feeling as if I was drowning in black waters. But I was back in the shed—and the witch ball was back in the chest.

"Opal!" I called out. "What just happened?"

I honestly do not know.

"Hortense must be crazy. You tried to help her and she wouldn't even listen. Those things she said about you were horrible."

Horrible . . . but not untrue.

"You can't mean . . . you couldn't!" I stopped, unable to finish.

Opal had been my closest friend, my companion since I was a little girl. She never spoke of her past, and when I asked she said that watching over me was all that mattered. I didn't care what happened in her past. I just loved having her with me always, my best friend forever.

What I did while on earth has nothing to do with you, she said softly. *The unfortunate details of my earth life are long buried.*

"So how did Hortense find out?"

That is something I do not know, but I shall look into this situation. I clearly underestimated her, and realize now she is a great danger. I never thought it possible to feel anything but peace here, but for the first time I feel fear—for you. Dearest Sabine, be safe until I return.

Then she was gone and I was alone—with the witch ball.

20

How could a bunch of glass look so pretty yet be so dangerous? It was hard to believe it was connected to evil—but I had no doubt of this and made sure the ball was locked securely in the chest before leaving the shed.

When I stepped outside, the clouds had passed and sunny rays shone down like a golden mist. I heard a squawk and saw Dagger circling overhead as Dominic strode over.

"What's going on?" Dominic furrowed his brow as he gestured to the building. "Were you in there?"

I nodded, guessing that Dagger squealed on me.

"You're shaking. You okay?"

"Define okay," I said with an attempt at a joke. But he didn't laugh, and gave me a deep look.

"We better talk," he said.

"I don't know . . . it's all really confusing."

"No rush. I've got to check the fence line for breaks. Walk with me."

"Well . . . all right." I wasn't sure why I went with him. Somehow it felt disloyal to Josh. All Dominic and I had in common was our desire to help Nona. So what if he had muscular shoulders, wavy hair that smelled fresh like woods, and amazingly gentle blue eyes? He wasn't a bad kisser either . . .

We walked along the edges of the pasture, and the silence stretched longer than the fence line. Without planning to, I found myself telling Dominic about my ghostly encounter in the shed. He never interrupted and I could tell he believed me. It felt good to share the weird part of my life with someone who understood. If only I could be as honest with Josh . . .

Conversation shifted to Nona and the missing remedy book. Dominic had a new lead on one of the names we'd gotten from Eleanor Baskers. He'd located a man from Arizona who might be a direct descendent of one of the sisters who had owned the charms.

"I might extend my trip to Nevada and check this guy out. I've left a message and should hear back in a few days," he added, bending over to tighten a loose strand of barbed wire on the fence.

A few days. A casual phrase that made my pulse quicken. Would I still be around in a few days?

I hid my uneasiness and complimented Dominic on finding more information. "It'll be great when we have all four charms," I added, breaking off a long piece of grass and twirling it around my finger. "Thanks for working on this."

"That's what I was hired to do."

"But you do it because you care about Nona."

"Sure, I do." He leaned close and gave me an intense look that hinted he cared about more than just my grandmother. My heart fluttered, and I told myself I was just imagining things. I mean, Dominic couldn't be flirting with me, that would just be too weird.

"Uh . . . thanks for all you've done to help Nona."

"I'll stay here long enough to make sure she's well."

"And then what?" I asked.

"I'll move on." There was something final in his tone that bothered me. It had never occurred to me that he would want to leave. He'd become such a part of our farm. Just seeing him around, working or hanging with the animals seemed natural; like he belonged here.

"A farm this size takes a lot of work," I told him. "Nona needs you around and won't want you to move away."

"I've never stayed anywhere long."

"Why not?"

"That's just how things are." He leaned against a fence post, his gaze drifting up to follow the falcon flying into the woods.

"So where will you go?"

"Wherever work takes me. I've been taking classes to be a farrier."

"A what?"

"Farrier—someone who shoes horses."

"I hope it works out for you." I twisted the piece of grass into a knot.

"You, too." He looked deeply into my face. "You don't have to worry about that witch ball. I've got the animals watching and nothing bad will happen."

He sounded confident, but I had my doubts— about a lot of things.

*　　*　　*

Wednesday dawned with bright skies and calm breezes. Not bad for what might be the second last day of my life, I thought morbidly.

I decided to have a positive attitude and make today the best ever.

I wore my best pair of embroidered jeans, a pink shirt Amy had given me for Christmas, and a dangly chain necklace I'd found at a flea market. I brushed my blond hair and fastened one side with a half-moon-shaped clip. Then I hurried downstairs to surprise Nona with a delicious breakfast of blueberry waffles, scrambled eggs, and orange juice.

Nona was surprised and grateful. Afterwards, she offered to do the dishes and told me to go ahead to school. So I left for school earlier than usual. I didn't really expect Josh to be at my locker yet. But I didn't expect to find someone else there waiting for me—Evan. He smiled in this smug, sly way, like a predator spying his victim.

"Hey, Sabine," he said casually as if we were friends.

I refused to reply. Lifting my head defiantly, I tried to walk around him to reach my locker. But he moved directly in front of me, one of those blocking moves his football fans admired.

"Did you like my card with the newspaper article?" he asked with a malicious glint in his eyes.

"Like isn't the word."

"You should thank me."

"Yeah, right," I said, glaring. "Thanks for being an asshole."

"Such harsh language! Josh would be shocked."

"You deserve worse. And leave Josh out of this."

"I've had plenty of chances to tell Josh about your witchy past."

"So why didn't you?"

He shrugged. "Didn't feel like it."

"And when will you feel like it?"

"Can't say. Why don't you tell me—you're the psychic."

"Move!" I dodged around him, but in a flash he was in front of me again.

"I can make a lot of trouble for you."

"Like you haven't already?"

"I haven't even started. You'd be smart to play nice."

Glaring, I retorted with the opposite of "nice." I mouthed off some fitting words I remembered reading on the bathroom wall.

"Is that the worst you can do?" he sneered.

"Give me time," I said with dark threat.

"Time is up." He gave a nasty laugh. "You need to be taught a lesson, so I've just decided that tonight I'm going to tell Josh. Everything." He leaned so close I could taste his hot breath. "And then I'll announce it to the whole school."

He laughed and turned away. As he strode off, I had vivid flash of him in a previous life. He was wearing a metal helmet, armed with sharp weapons, and riding on a ship in foggy waters, on a quest to pillage villages and torture innocent people. Hundreds of years hadn't improved his personality. And not-so-lucky-me was his latest victim. Only now his sharpest weapon was his mouth.

I hated how he played me. All that time he hung out with Josh, knowing I'd imagine the worst. He hoped I'd squirm and bleed like a worm stabbed on a hook. He was clever, I'll give him credit for that. By saying nothing to Josh, he'd prolonged my anxiety. He probably let his boat drift away on purpose. I'll bet Evan had the ignition keys on him the whole time. He'd been toying with me, but now he meant business, and he would tell Josh tonight.

Unless I beat him to it.

21

During lunch, Josh wanted to sit with Evan and some other friends. I'd rather sit with Penny-Love and the cheerleaders. We compromised and sat at a table between the two groups, far enough to shut Evan out of our conversation, but too close to discuss anything private. I caught Evan smirking at me, and shot him a defiant glare.

So I invited Josh to come to my house after school and stay for dinner. I'd always tried to keep my school and home separate, so this was the first time I'd ever invited him and he eagerly accepted.

Take that, Evan! I thought in triumph.

I called Nona to let her know about dinner. She was a thousand percent behind me and even offered to spend the evening with her poker pal Grady so Josh and I could be alone.

When I walked into my last-period class, Manny rushed over excitedly. "Guess what?" he asked, his dark eyes shining. "I saw *him.*"

"Him?" I blinked.

"K.C.!"

"No way! Are you serious?"

Manny's black dreads swayed as he nodded. "He must have slipped into my class when I wasn't looking. When the bell rang, I stood to grab my stuff and there he was! Sitting in the back behind this hulking dude from the wrestling team."

"How could you be sure he was K.C.?"

"Because he looked so . . . so ordinary—average height, average face, average hair. I can't even describe him. I still don't remember him from the festival, but he seemed to recognize me. When he caught me looking, he took off. I went after him, only he was too fast. I remembered his schedule and

checked his next class before I came here, but no
K.C."

"Why is he so scared?" I wondered. "His aunt
acted afraid, too."

"Don't know, but I'm going to find out,"
Manny said with determination.

I trusted Manny and knew he'd succeed. I just
hoped it happened before tomorrow.

Manny went over to his desk and I sat down
at my usual computer. This week's *Sheridan Shout-
Out* had just come out and already I was swamped
with articles to edit for next week's issue. There
was my other secret work, too—the predictions I
gave Manny for his column. Of course, the last
thing I felt like doing now was coming up with
predictions.

After editing a few articles, I opened up a notebook and started planning my menu for tonight—
and my talk with Josh. It would be best to present
things in a scientific manner. I'd go online and
print out lots of psychic facts—not the skeptical
stuff, but the factual research. There are many paranormal research foundations, and countries like
Russia have long respected psychics. When you
considered all the unexplained things in this world,

it made more sense to accept the existence of the other side. I could even show Josh statistics that proved aliens were real . . . but I didn't want to push my luck.

When the last bell rang, I gathered my papers and shoved them into my backpack. Then I joined the throng of kids heading for the door. Josh and I had agreed to meet by my locker, and I wanted to get there first.

"Sabine," Manny called, coming up beside me. "Did you finish proofing that article on music downloads?"

"Not yet." I slipped my backpack over my shoulders as we moved into the hall and kids swarmed around us. "I'll do it tomorrow."

"Good enough. Talk to you—" He gasped and pointed. "IT'S HIM!"

I followed his gaze and saw a medium-height kid with brown hair, wearing jeans and a tan T-shirt. A totally average-looking guy.

"K.C.!" I shouted.

He turned and met my gaze with a stark look of terror. Then he spun around and ran away.

Manny took off running, and I was running, too. We pushed through a group of girls in band uniforms, then turned a corner. I kept thinking of Manny's predictions and how K.C. was my last chance at proving one of them wrong. It was a wild hope with no basis of logic. But logic didn't have much to do with ghosts anyway. If K.C.'s prediction didn't come true, it would mean the witch ball wasn't that powerful.

We seemed to be heading for the school parking lot, and Manny burst forward with amazing speed. I couldn't keep up, but I was able to keep him in sight.

"He's getting into that gray Chevy!" Manny yelled to me.

"He'll get away!"

"Not if we hurry. Go to my car!"

Everything happened so fast. Car doors flung open, we scrambled inside, grabbing for seat belts and buckling in tight. The engine roared to life, wheels squealed, and we zoomed out of the parking lot.

Manny floored it in pursuit. My elbow banged against the door as the gray car made a sharp right. We sped forward, zipping through a yellow light to keep up. The other car changed lanes and disappeared behind a truck.

"Get out of the way!" Manny swore at the truck.

As if the driver could hear him, the truck turned into a grocery store parking lot. But there was no sign of the gray car.

"Where did he—" Manny started to say.

"There!" I pointed at a gray blur making a left turn. "He's trying to lose you."

"Almost did, too. Great navigating, Beany."

"Thanks! But don't call me . . . Hey, I think he's headed to the freeway."

"I hope not," Manny said with a worried frown. "My car shakes at 65, so it would be hard to keep up. Besides I can't afford to get another speeding ticket."

"Another ticket?" I teased.

"Don't ask." He groaned.

"Look!" I suddenly cried out, swiveling to gesture out the window. "He passed the onramp and he's making a U-turn!"

"I'm on it. Hold tight!" Manny spun the wheel, and only our seatbelts kept us from slamming into each other.

"What's with him anyway?" I complained as I rubbed my sore arm. "Why is he so desperate to get away?"

But Manny was too busy dodging traffic to answer. The gray car snaked in and out of lanes and Manny kept close behind. He clenched his teeth, sweat beading on his forehead and a determined gleam in his dark eyes. He made a sharp turn into a residential neighborhood.

"I know this area," I said. "Danielle lives around here. I think this street dead ends at a park."

"Good. That guy is driving like a maniac!"

"He's afraid," I said with a sudden insight. I couldn't see K.C., but for a moment I *felt* him and had a jumble of mental images: a graveyard, jail bars, a rolled sleeping bag, and the letter "W."

"We've got him!" Manny exclaimed, pumping his free arm in the air. "He's gonna have to stop for that school bus up ahead and there are no side streets. Unless he can fly, he's trapped with no way out."

I let out the breath I hadn't realized I was holding, glad this crazy chase was coming to an end. A block away I saw flashing red lights on a bulky, yellow bus. I used to ride a bus like that when I lived in San Jose—back when Mom worked a day job. But when the twins started modeling, Mom quit to manage their careers. My sisters never had to ride a crowded bus; Mom was their chauffeur.

"What's that idiot doing?"

I glanced over at Manny who was staring ahead in jaw-dropping disbelief. I followed his gaze and felt my own jaw drop. The gray car wasn't slowing down! It barreled forward, ignoring the bus's flashing lights and zooming directly for the bus driver as she escorted three little kids across the street.

The bus driver started running, grabbing and pushing the kids to the sidewalk. At the same time K.C. must have realized the danger because there was a screech of brakes. The car skidded and swerved, burning tread as it spun around in a dizzy circle.

Everything happened so fast.

The kids and bus driver were safely on the sidewalk while the gray car faced the opposite direction. I glimpsed pale fear on K.C.'s face as he shifted the car back into gear, hit the gas, then rocketed past us.

Manny groaned and smacked the steering wheel. "Damn! We almost had him!"

"At least no one was hurt," I pointed out, watching the bus crank back up, fold its doors, then rumble off in a smoky stench of diesel.

"I blew it." Manny checked his mirrors and followed the speed limit.

"It wasn't your fault. Maybe we can still catch him."

"How?"

"Three guesses where he's headed?"

"I'll need more than three." Manny looked at me, slowly realization dawned. "Oh—the apartment."

I nodded. "It's worth a try."

So we headed back to the apartment building, scanning the parking lot as we drove in. There were two gray cars, but neither of them looked quite right. "I think his gray car had a broken tail light," I said, wishing I'd been paying closer attention.

"The license plate started with WYW," Manny said.

Even though we couldn't find K.C.'s car, we decided to check his apartment. This time we both went to the door, and my heart dropped when the aunt answered our knock. She wasn't happy to see me either and snapped, "He's still not here!"

"I wish she wouldn't slam the door so hard," I said as we turned away. "My ears are ringing. Now what?"

For the first time in my short history with Manny, he didn't have an answer. I didn't have one either. So we walked back, our footsteps heavy. We had almost reached the stairs when I heard running feet.

"Wait!" a young voice called.

Turning, I saw a little girl with long, brown hair and bright yellow sneakers. "How come you're looking for my brother?" she asked, breathing heavy.

Excitement rose in Manny's face. He went over and knelt down by the little girl. "Brother? Do you mean K.C.?"

She nodded solemnly.

"Zoey," I guessed, offering a friendly smile. "I'm Sabine and he's Manny."

She nodded again, giving me a shy smile. "I heard you tell Aunt Felicia you go to school with K.C."

"He's in my class," Manny said. "But he's hard to find sometimes. Can you tell us where he is?"

"I could, only I'm not supposed to talk about him."

"But we're his friends," Manny assured, flashing a warm, dimpled grin.

"I'm not supposed to run in the halls, but I do it anyway." She glanced behind cautiously, then put her finger to her lips and told us where K.C. worked.

22

I felt triumphant as we drove away from the apartment—until I glanced down at my watch. Then I nearly died.

"Ohmygod! It's after four!"

"So?" Manny asked.

"I was supposed to meet Josh at my locker."

"Doubt he's still there," Manny said wryly, slowing for a stoplight. "But I can take you if you want to check."

"What's the use?" I put my hands over my face and moaned. Josh must totally hate me! And he would never accept my reason for standing him up. Chasing after a ghost's prediction was *not* logical.

Damage control was needed—and fast. If I could talk to Josh, I'd tell him I'd been out on a newspaper assignment with Manny. No reason to mention ghosts or predictions. But when I pulled out my cell phone from my backpack, I groaned. I wasn't used to having a phone yet and had forgotten to recharge the battery. It was dead—like how I felt inside.

"Take me home," I said grimly.

"Sure, Sabine."

As we pulled into the long driveway, I had an unrealistic hope that I'd find Josh here waiting for me. I glanced around for his car. But there were no cars parked by the yellow country home, not even Nona's. I remembered she was over at Grady's, playing poker so I could be alone with Josh.

Numbly, I told Manny I'd see him later.

"Yeah, at 10:30. And about Josh—" He reached out to pat my shoulder. "It'll be okay."

"Yeah," I replied with zero confidence.

Stepping into the house, my footsteps echoed on the tiled entry. I found a note from Nona propped in a fruit basket on the table. "Chicken defrosting and fresh corn in fridge. You two lovebirds have fun," she wrote.

Crossing to the counter, I reached to pick up the phone, then paused when I noticed the message light flashing and saw there were three messages. Instantly, I had a bad feeling. Like I should turn away now, before it was too late. But I couldn't ignore the red message light, and pushed the "listen" button.

The first message was from a very cheerful mortgage lender who had a wonderful deal to offer that would change our lives in amazing ways.

Click. Erase.

The second was from my sister Amy, asking me to check my email as soon as I got home.

I'd check later. Click. Erase.

The final call was Josh; his tone was cold. "Sabine, I waited at our locker, but you never showed. Then Zach tells me you drove off with Manny. What's that about? I thought I could trust you. Guess not. Don't call back. I'm headed over to Evan's."

A heavy click. The message ended.

And that wasn't all that was ending.

My heart hurt so much, I wanted to crawl under my covers and never come out. I had so blown it with Josh. Being his girl always seemed like a miracle, like I'd really made it at Sheridan High. Other kids respected Josh for his athletic skill and all-around-nice-guy attitude. Not to mention the fact he was totally gorgeous.

So why did I go and ruin everything?

I put the defrosted chicken in the fridge, and pulled out a carton of mocha-toffee ice cream. I didn't bother getting a bowl, and ate it directly from the carton. When my brain started to freeze, I put the ice cream away and went to my room.

Sorting through my CDs, I ignored all the trendy artists that Penny-Love raved about, and settled on soothing ocean sounds. I tried to do homework. My mind strayed when I glanced at my dresser and saw a picture of Josh and me that Penny-Love had taken with her digital camera. The angle of the camera was just right, so my blond hair fell in shiny waves that hid the stripe of black that was a family trait of a seer. I looked as happy and normal as any girl with the guy she loved.

And I so loved being Josh's girl. Was that the same as being in love with him? I wondered, as I opened a cupboard in the wall and pulled out my craft bag. Emotions were so confusing—guilt, hurt, anger, shame. I didn't even blame Josh for being mad. I totally deserved it. I shouldn't have ditched him to rush off with Manny. Josh would never do that to me. I didn't deserve him. I never could figure out why he chose me anyway—we were so different. Maybe breaking up was inevitable.

Leaning back against my pillows, I worked on my embroidery. Reddish brown thread wove in and out, the needle like a quicksilver fish slipping through waves of fabric. A bushy-tailed fox took shape, then a snowy hill. My fingers moved automatically, my gaze lifting to the window where the sky was a gloomy sea of gray. Even the oak trees seemed to shiver, spindly branches bare of leaves. Although my room was heated, I felt chilled and huddled underneath my blankets.

I must have fallen asleep because when I lifted my head and looked out the window, it was dark. My embroidery and thread had fallen to the floor. Glancing at my clock, I was surprised to find it was after eight. No surprise my stomach felt queasy; ice cream didn't make a satisfying dinner.

Downstairs, Nona had come back home and bragged about beating the buttons off Grady at cards. They used a jar full of old buttons instead of money or poker chips. When she asked about my dinner with Josh, I told her he couldn't make it, but I avoided any further explanation by saying I was going to make a sandwich. Then I hurried away from her curious eyes and into the kitchen.

I was relieved when Nona went to bed early, leaving the coast clear for me to sneak out with Manny. Slipping on a jacket, I waited by the mailbox until I saw the approaching headlights of his car.

"Hop in," he said, opening the passenger door and gesturing for me to get inside.

"Okay." Now that I was actually doing this, I had second thoughts. Like maybe chasing after a weird guy was a bad idea. I'd rather be safe and snug in bed. But I doubted I'd sleep well anyway, and would end up with nightmares.

Soon we were leaving Sheridan Valley and on the freeway headed north. K.C. had a job at a super Wal-Mart. According to his sister, he stocked shelves.

Entering the well-lit store felt like going from night into day. I was surprised to find so many customers this late. I'd expected the store to be quiet like the school halls after hours, but instead all kinds of people were shopping, even mothers pushing little kids in carts.

After asking around, we headed to the rear of the store and entered a door marked Employees Only.

"Target sighted," Manny said in a low voice.

I recognized K.C. right away. He wore a uniform with a store logo and name badge. He was stacking boxes with his back turned to us. Manny and I whispered together, deciding that I would go forward while Manny circled around and blocked K.C. from running again.

While Manny slipped behind some boxes, I watched K.C. as he worked, paying close attention to his aura. He moved with his head down, his brown hair falling across his face. I expected to see bland colors, but he glowed with soft, lovely pastels, much brighter than the average person.

Cautiously, I stepped forward and spoke gently, "Hi K.C."

He turned, panic flaring on his face and I could tell he was ready to run. So I offered a comforting smile and said quickly, "Wait. Please don't go."

"What do you want?" He clutched a box.

"To talk to you."

"I got nothing to say. Leave me alone."

"I'll leave as soon as you answer one question," I spoke gently.

But he was sharp with suspicion. "What question?"

"About the school carnival. You were there, weren't you?"

"Maybe I was, what's it to you?"

"You went to Mystic Manny."

His eyes narrowed. "That's why you look so familiar. I saw you with Mystic Manny. Why were you chasing me?"

"So we could talk about his prediction for you."

"Really?" he asked curiously. "That's all he wants?"

I nodded solemnly.

"Well . . . okay." He relaxed his grip on the box, setting it on the floor. "I felt bad about ditching Manny. I respect him and all—I just don't want him writing about me."

"He won't," I assured.

"Better not. I like things private."

I nodded, understanding this all too well.

"I'll take my lunch break early, so we can talk somewhere quieter." He raised his voice as the ground rumbled and a mini-forklift roared by.

It seemed weird to take a lunch break at night. Since K.C. seemed more relaxed now, I confessed that Manny was waiting nearby.

"He's here?"

"Yeah. We came together."

"Well . . . okay. But he better not use his mystic powers on me."

Powers? It took all my control not to laugh. I thought maybe he was joking until I looked at his expression. Totally serious.

"Manny won't do anything mystic." I lifted my hand solemnly. "I promise."

A few minutes later, the three of us were heading towards a back exit on the way to K.C.'s car so he could get his sack lunch. As we walked, K.C. glanced at Manny with a look of awe. "Sorry for running from you before."

"It's okay, man."

"I never miss your column and it blows me away how you know so much. But what do you want from me? Your powers tell you anything you need to know."

"Not always." Manny's dreads swayed as he tilted his head. "Using my . . . er . . . abilities takes a lot of concentration so I have to conserve my energy."

K.C. nodded. "Oh, that explains it."

"It does?" Manny asked, surprised.

We reached the exit door, and I glanced at K.C. who was regarding Manny with admiration and awe.

"Sure. You watch out for the people who get your predictions. But don't worry about me, it turned out okay."

"Uh . . . great." Manny paused, his hand on the doorknob. "What exactly happened?"

"Like you don't already know. Your prediction was so accurate, it already happened,"

"It did?" I asked in a choked whisper.

"Yeah—weeks ago. I got things under control now, and no one knew—except Manny. He nailed my prediction."

I felt like walls were closing in on me, and I needed some air. I pushed past Manny and yanked open the door, rushing outside. Only a dim bulb above the door brightened the black night. Darkness closed in, shadows shifting like silent watchers.

Chilly air made me shiver and I clutched my jacket tightly around me.

"Beany, you okay?" Manny asked as he and K.C. came up beside me, the door banging shut behind them.

I bent over slightly, catching my breath. "I-I'm fine."

"Panic attack?" K.C. guessed with a sympathetic look. "I know how bad they can be. Breathe in and out till you calm down."

"I just want to know about your prediction," I said weakly.

"It can wait till you feel better."

"No." I shook my head. "Now."

K.C. glanced uncertainly at Manny. "Didn't you fill her in?"

"Not yet." Manny shook his head. "My readings are all confidential. I wanted to talk to you first since I respect the privacy of my clients."

K.C. nodded, like this completely made sense. And I realized that Manny did have super powers. He was a master at B.S.

We stood on the cement landing, my hand closing around a cold metal railing as K.C. began to talk. "I always read Manny's column, but I didn't know how major his powers were till the carnival," he explained. "His crystal ball glowed with real magic. He went into a trance and told me, 'You will suffer isolation when you lose your home.' It was like—wow! He knew all about us getting evicted when Mom had to go away."

Thinking back on my conversation with his aunt, I mentally translated "go away" as being arrested and sent to jail.

"Tough break," Manny said. "So you had to move in with your aunt?"

"How did you know that? Of course—the power thing." K.C. slapped his forehead, then added with awe, "You really do know everything."

"But you had already lost your house before the prediction," I pointed out. "Manny said you *would* lose your home, not that you *had* lost it. Technically the prediction didn't come true."

"Manny was close enough."

I didn't argue, although I felt as if a huge weight had been lifted. The witch ball ghost hadn't been one hundred percent accurate. If she'd only been "close" this time, she could be wrong about my prediction.

We kept walking to the parking lot. Finding out some good news gave me hope for more good news. Tomorrow I'd see Josh at school and I'd finally find the courage to tell him about my past. It wouldn't be easy, but I'd make him understand that a psychic gift wasn't that different than inheriting a talent for music or art. Even if he never believed in ghosts, he'd at least know I was really sorry for standing him up.

I was imagining being surrounded by friends who applauded while Josh and I shared this really romantic make-up kiss, when a sharp cry jerked my thoughts back to the parking lot.

"It's gone!" K.C.'s hand flew to his pale face.

"What's gone?" Manny and I both asked.

"My car!" K.C. pointed to an empty space between two trucks. "It was right here!"

"Are you sure?" Manny asked, swiveling his head to look around.

"Positive! I was nervous after you chased me, so I parked out of sight between these two trucks. I usually park closer . . . Ohmygod! This can't be happening! Not my car!"

"Hey, take it easy. You'll get it back," Manny assured, patting his shoulder. "Call it in right away so the police can start looking."

"The police?" K.C. shook his head. "No! Not them! They'll make me go back to—" He cut off abruptly.

"To what?" Manny asked.

"My aunt. And I'd rather die. I totally hate her!" His dark eyes burned. "No one can make me go back there. You don't know what she's like!"

"I have a good idea," I said grimly. "But I'm confused here. She told me you lived with her."

"That's what she wants everyone to think. She goes on about how kind she was to take in two kids, but she's only in it for the support money she gets. Not that she uses it for us. We fought a lot until I couldn't take it anymore and split."

"Where do you live now?" I asked.

"Nowhere. My car wasn't just a car—" His voice cracked. Miserably, he pointed at the empty parking space. "My car was my home. And it's gone."

23

THURSDAY

K.C. had lost his home—just as Manny predicted.

Manny offered K.C. some money, but he refused. For a guy with next to nothing, he had a lot of pride. He said he'd get by, and watch out for his sister, too. Turns out he secretly passed on money to her for clothes and school supplies.

"If you want to help me," K.C. told Manny. "Use your powers to find my car."

Manny hesitated, then he said solemnly, "I'll do my best."

"Thanks." There was nothing average about K.C. as he lifted his chin, straightened his shoulders, and said he'd better get back to work.

On the drive to my house, Manny didn't say much and seemed focused on the road. I thought he was worrying about K.C., but I was wrong.

"That makes three," he said in the most serious tone I'd ever heard from him.

"Three?"

"Predictions. I could ignore one or even two— but three is beyond coincidence."

"It doesn't mean anything." I spoke confidently, but to be honest, I was getting scared. It was freaky how the predictions only came true *after* I got involved. My presence made it possible for Jill to see a ghost, Jacques stepped in the oil while talking to me, and K.C.'s car had been parked in a hidden spot after Manny and I had chased him. The common denominator each time was *me*.

Manny slowed the car to a stop sign, an odd expression playing on his dark face. He sucked in a deep breath as he turned towards me. "Drastic means are required."

I arched an eyebrow. "How drastic?"

"Beany, can I sleep with you tonight?"

"What!" I couldn't have been more shocked if he'd announced he was going to shave his head, give up girls, and live in Tibet.

"Hear me out. You need someone to get you through tomorrow. I'll stay close and watch out for you. You don't have anything to worry about—it's not like I'm after your body."

"Gee, thanks," I said sarcastically.

"That didn't come out right." Manny slapped his forehead. "I mean, you have a hot body, but I think of you as a friend not a girl. Okay, that came out wrong, too."

I wasn't sure whether to smack him or laugh.

Brave soul, he tried again. "What I'm offering is to be your bodyguard."

"I can guard my own body—thank you very much," I told him firmly. "Nothing is going to happen."

"You can't ignore the powers of my predictions."

"They weren't *your* predictions. They're from a pathetic ghost named Hortense. Anyway, I have no plans to die tomorrow."

"Check your watch. It's already tomorrow."

I looked down at my wrist and shivered. Seven after midnight.

But I shrugged it all off. I wasn't going to change my life because of a disturbed ghost. Hortense couldn't hurt me. Her only power was in causing fear, just like Evan. Neither of them could win if I refused to be afraid.

"Those predictions are harmless," I told Manny.

"I'm not willing to take that chance." His hands tightened around the steering wheel as he accelerated. "I'll sleep on the floor if I have to, but I'm going to make sure you're protected for the next twenty-four hours."

By the time we reached my home, we'd reached a compromise. Manny could stay the night, but not in my bedroom. I went to get blankets and a pillow so he'd be comfortable on the couch.

I expected a restless sleep, but I was so exhausted, I fell asleep immediately. I only woke up once, after dreaming that I was watching car races, only to find out the motor I heard was from the purring of my cat Lilybelle. She curled up against me and I fell back asleep to her rumbling purr.

When I awoke, I was surprised to find out it was after nine. I couldn't believe that I had slept that late on a school day. Why hadn't Nona woken me?

Jumping up, I rushed around my room searching for shoes, a clean pair of jeans, and a T-shirt. I twisted my hair in a ponytail, only giving it a quick brushing, and skipped applying makeup. Then I grabbed my backpack, raced downstairs—and found Manny and Thorn sitting at the dining table.

I stared in astonishment. "Where's my grandmother?"

"Out running errands," Manny said casually, like nothing was unusual and I woke up every day to find these two having breakfast at my home.

"Manny is a great cook," Thorn said after swallowing. "These are the best pancakes I've had in ages."

"Thanks. It's the blueberries and vanilla."

"Excellent combo. Yumm!"

"Would you like more?" Manny said, offering a plate of steaming pancakes. When she shook her head, he turned to me. "How about you, Beany?"

I stomped over to the table. "Why aren't you at school? What's going on here?"

"Breakfast," Thorn answered, reaching for a glass of orange juice. She wore a longish pink-and-black wig, black lipstick, and a pink leather dog collar with silver studs. "Are you always this grumpy in the morning?"

"I am not grumpy. But I smell conspiracy."

"Not a conspiracy. This is an intervention." Manny eased me into a chair at the table. "Beany, you're under house arrest."

"Forget it." I tried to stand, only he was stronger. "Move. I'm going to school."

"No," Manny said firmly. "You're staying here today."

"Your grandmother agrees it's a good idea," Thorn added.

"Nona's in on this?" I asked indignantly.

"Two hundred percent," Thorn said, lifting up two mauve-tipped fingers. "She's buying snacks and renting videos to keep you comfortable. She already called the school to report you sick. And I talked to Dominic, too."

I groaned. "You didn't!"

She nodded proudly. "He's keeping an eye on things outside."

It was a conspiracy! I remembered my cat in my room last night and the glimpse of wings out my window. His animal posse was spying on me.

I tried to stand up, only Manny kept a firm hold on my shoulders. "Let me go. I can't miss school."

"I knew she'd be difficult," Thorn said, wiping syrup from her chin.

"I have a right to be. You can't keep me here like a prisoner."

"Watch us," Manny said ominously.

"I'm leaving now!"

"We'll see about that." Manny reached into his pocket and lunged forward. He grabbed my arm and there was a flash of silver. I heard the sound of metal clinking as he pulled my arm behind my back. Then before I knew what was happening, he slipped a handcuff on my wrist. He fastened the other half to a chair.

"Take this off!" I shouted, jerking my arm and only managing to move the chair a few inches. The skin around my wrist burned and so did I. "This is not funny! Unlock me now!"

Manny pursed his lips stubbornly and stepped out of my reach. "Beany, you're not going anywhere until this day is over."

Thorn stood beside him with her arms folded across her chest. "We're your guards, whether you like it or not."

I didn't like it. Not one little bit. Especially since I desperately needed to get to school so I could see Josh. I had to talk with him today; tomorrow would be too late. Evan would make sure of that. This was too personal to discuss with Manny or Thorn, so I used every other argument I could think of to convince them to give up their plan.

But they remained firm. I was so mad, I could hardly think straight. Part of me was also grateful that they cared enough to make me miserable. They were impossible—and wonderful. I hated and loved them.

Ultimately, I gave in. They made me swear on my grandmother's life that I would not sneak off to school. I'd never go back on that solemn oath—and they knew it. I had lost . . . more than they knew.

All the fight was out of me as Manny unlocked the cuff.

"That's more like it." He handed me a printed paper. "Now let's get down to business. Here's your schedule."

"My what?" I asked.

"Schedule," Manny said.

Taking the paper, I stared at it with dismay. My life was organized into hours and bodyguards.

12AM-8AM: Manny
8AM-10AM: Manny/Thorn
10AM-12PM: Thorn/Nona
12PM-3PM: Nona
3PM-7PM: Thorn
7PM-Midnight: Manny/Nona

There was also a list of rules. My jailers wouldn't allow me to do anything on my own. "No sharp objects, being near machinery, deep water, eating anything we don't try first, or lifting heavy objects."

It was worse than being in prison.

But a solemn swear was unbreakable, so I surrendered to my friends. After cleaning away breakfast dishes, we hung out in the living room. Manny filled Thorn in on last night, making the car chase sound like something out of an action movie and K.C. come off like a tragic hero. Then Manny's shift was over and he headed to school to catch up his newspaper duties.

"Not fair!" I complained. "Manny gets to go to school and I'm stuck here."

Thorn busted up laughing. "Never knew anyone mad about missing school."

"No one handcuffs me at school," I said accusingly, rubbing my bruised wrist.

Before leaving, Manny offered to pick up my assignments and asked if I wanted him to pass on messages to anyone.

After a long pause, I shook my head.

Thorn and I sorted through DVDs, debating what to watch. With everything going on, I wasn't in the mood for a thriller or a romance. Finally we chose an adventure flick which kept my mind off Josh. When it ended and I glanced at the clock, I wondered what was keeping Nona.

"Are you sure she only went to the grocery store?" I asked Thorn.

"Yeah. She said she wouldn't be gone long."

"She must have stopped somewhere else." I frowned, trying to imagine what could have kept her for over three hours. "I'll call her. I hope she remembered to take her cell phone."

She had—but the connection echoed and Nona's voice sounded weird.

"Sabine, where are you?" she asked, her words echoing.

"At home."

"Why aren't you in school?"

"Nona, you called the school to say I was sick."

A hesitation, then she said almost accusingly, "You don't sound sick."

"I'm not . . . Don't you remember?"

"Remember what?" Her voice rose in panic. "Everything is confusing."

"Where exactly are you?"

"I-I don't know." Her voice broke. "I'm sitting in my car on a street I've never seen before . . . I have no idea how I got here. Sabine, I'm lost."

24

My worst fears for my grandmother were coming true—despite her seeming so much better lately. I'd started to believe she could beat her illness even without the remedy. The more she talked, the more confused she sounded. She couldn't tell me where she was, and I didn't recognize nearby streets or businesses.

Finally, it was Thorn who took charge. She got on the phone and asked Nona questions. While she listened, her eyes glazed over and I knew she was tuning into her finding skill. Her energy swirled, reaching out like a radar to Nona. After a few minutes, she told my grandmother she was on her way. Thorn sounded confident that she could bring my grandmother home.

But I shared none of her confidence when I found out that Thorn had asked Dominic to watch me while she was gone. When he joined me in the living room, I felt oddly tongue-tied. I sat on the couch, drawing my legs up under me.

He stood in front of me, making no move to sit down. "So how you holding up?" he asked, shoving his hands in his pockets.

"Okay." I managed to sound casual.

"Good." He just stood there as if waiting for me to say more. Even with the TV on, the room seemed unnaturally silent.

"This is all so unnecessary," I finally said with a frustrated wave of my arm. "The witch ball is locked up and can't cause any more trouble. I do *not* need a babysitter."

"Better safe than dead."

"Nothing is going to happen to me. Manny and Thorn overreacted. I should be at school right now, and you probably have chores to finish."

He shook his head. "Already done."

"What about your horseshoe classes?"

"Not until tomorrow."

"You must have better things to do than hang around here."

"Nope."

"Well I do. This is all messed up."

"It'll be better by tomorrow."

"For me maybe—but not Nona. I still can't believe she got lost. Little kids get lost, not grown women." The drone of the TV rattled my nerves, so I grasped the remote control and shut off the power. "She's getting worse and we're no closer to finding the remedy book."

"Not so." He sat down on the other end of the couch. "I heard back from that guy in Arizona. His name and info fits, and he claims to have old family jewelry."

"Including silver charms?" I asked hopefully.

"He thinks so, but it's in storage and he can't check till after work. He'll get back to me then, so we may have the remedy soon."

"That would be so great!" I almost reached out to hug him—until sanity clicked in and I jerked my arms back.

"Do I make you uncomfortable?" He flashed a wicked smile and scooted close to me—way too close.

"Of course not. I'm totally at ease. Why would you even ask?"

"Because you're clawing that pillow."

I hadn't realized I was holding a pillow. When I looked down and saw the fabric ripping under my fingernails, I tossed the pillow on the floor. "I'm fine."

"No argument there."

His gaze fixed on me. Instead of turning away, which would have been the smart thing to do, I met his gaze, and emotions sizzled so sharp and overwhelming, I could hardly breathe. Warmth spread through me and I felt lightheaded. I thought of Josh, who probably hated me by now. I wasn't sure how Dominic felt towards me—except I knew for sure it was definitely not hate.

He leaned closer . . .

"I-I'd better watch TV," I said, panicked.

I jumped off the couch, tripping over the pillow I'd tossed on the carpet. I steadied myself, then sat far away from Dominic in the recliner, aiming the remote at the screen. Click, click . . . I flipped through channels like a maniac, switching fast if I came to anything romantic. Finally I settled on a documentary about cockroaches.

Turns out I couldn't have picked a better show for Dominic. Who knew he'd find cockroaches so interesting? Or maybe whatever chemistry flared between us made him as uncomfortable as it made me, and he was relieved to change the mood.

The documentary was nearly over when Thorn returned with my grandmother. Nona didn't say a word about getting lost, and went directly into the kitchen where she put on a teakettle.

Thorn was running late and had to leave. Dominic tactfully excused himself, too, so it was just Nona and me.

"Can I help?" I asked my grandmother, coming to sit beside her at the kitchen table where she was digging through a box of assorted herbal tea bags.

"Don't coddle me." She lifted her chin defiantly. "I am competent enough to pour my own tea."

"Of course you are. Can I have a cup, too?"

"Wild berry, peppermint, or cinnamon spice?"

"Peppermint. Thanks, Nona," I added, reaching out to put my arm around her slim shoulders. She felt so warm and secure, and I needed her so much. She'd always been the one to protect me from the shadows and spirits I saw at night. I couldn't bear to lose her.

The teakettle whistled and for a few minutes the only sound was the clicking of our spoons as we stirred our cups. Spice and mint scents warmed the kitchen, and I felt calmer.

"Sorry for scaring you," Nona told me. "But I'm fine now, so don't worry about me. I'm more worried about you."

"Don't be."

"The moment you brought that witch ball into this house, I sensed it meant trouble. I should have made you get rid of it right away."

"Dominic locked it up, so it can't cause any problems." I didn't add about my encounter with Hortense. That would only cause Nona more concern.

"Predictions from dark entities must never be taken lightly. Your friends told me about the other three predictions."

"That was just a fluke." To change the subject, I told her about Dominic's results searching for the remedy book. "He may have tracked down another charm. So we might have the remedy soon."

"That would be a relief."

"Then you'll be well."

"I hope so. But at the moment, I'm more concerned about you." She kissed my cheek. "According to Manny's schedule, it's my shift."

I rolled my eyes at the mention of the "schedule." But Nona suggested using our time to bake caramel chip cookies, and who was I to argue?

Being under house arrest never tasted so delicious. Nona kept smacking my hand away from the batter, but I told her it was the best part. We laughed as she shaped dough and inhaled the delicious scent of baking cookies. I was glad to shut off worries and just have fun.

Around two o'clock, I got a call from Thorn, apologizing because she was running late. "Ask Nona or Dominic to cover for me till I get there," she said in a rushed voice.

"Why? What's up?"

"After you told me about K.C., I couldn't stop thinking about him. I've been to homeless shelters with my mom and it's always heartbreaking. So I talked to K.C. and said I'd help find his car."

"If anyone can, it's you."

"Can't hurt to try. Although I didn't tell him how I'd look—that's not something I want getting around. Besides, I can't guarantee it'll work."

I wished her luck, then we hung up.

I probably should have let Nona know Thorn was delayed, but I didn't. My grandmother was busy in her office, and I saw no reason to disturb her. Besides, the day was already half over and nothing had happened. This confirmed my theory that since the witch ball was locked away, I was safe.

Finding quiet time alone, I wasn't sure what to do. TV was boring and I couldn't concentrate on computer games. I wandered into my room and pulled out my craft bag, deciding to start a new project. Sorting through my supplies, I pulled out a skein of variegated orange-red yarn perfect for knitting Nona a scarf. She appreciated homemade gifts, unlike my mom. After finding a pair of slippers I'd crocheted for Mom in the Goodwill box, I never made her anything again.

Mom was like a burr that stuck to me, and hard to shake off. Sitting on my bed, I stared out the window, wondering how I could love my mom even though she drove me crazy. Emotions were complicated, I guess. Like how Jill felt about her father. She still suffered because of him, even though he was dead. I think she wanted to hate him, and he definitely deserved it, but she loved him, too. My sisters were dealing with love-hate issues, too. The twin bond that united them now seemed to be ripping them apart. Love and hate were opposites, yet the same.

How was I supposed to know about my own feelings? Dominic continued to confuse me, shifting from dark to light moods. I was intrigued by him, yet frustrated, too. I couldn't exactly call him a friend, so what kind of relationship did we have? And what about Josh? Did we still have a relationship?

If only I'd gone to school this morning. Here I was, ready to be totally honest with him, and I lost my chance because of a stupid prediction. That damn witch ball! Nona was right about it causing trouble. That's all it had done since I brought it home. I wanted to go to the shed right now and smash it, destroy it so completely it could never hurt anyone again. But was that even possible? What would happen if I destroyed the ball? Would Hortense seek revenge on me?

My thoughts chased themselves in a dizzy circle. I just wanted to shut off everything. I unraveled some orange-red yarn and reached for my knitting needles. I was on my third row—when the phone rang.

Dropping needles and yarn, I grabbed it quickly so it wouldn't disturb Nona.

"Sabine, have you seen her?" It was my mother and she sounded panicked.

"Seen who?"

"Amy. She's—" Mom broke off with a sob. "She's run away."

25

Sometime after Mom dropped my sisters off at school, Amy had left. Classmates didn't remember seeing her. Her teacher assumed she was absent. Apparently last night Amy and Ashley had a "minor disagreement" (as Mom put it), and weren't speaking. They had different schedules, so she figured Amy was avoiding her.

I told Mom I hadn't heard anything and promised to let her know if I did.

My first impulse was to rush downstairs and tell Nona. But was that really a good idea? Nona had been so shaken by getting lost, and this could trigger another episode. There wasn't much to tell anyway. Amy would show up soon and then all the worry would be for nothing.

Where would Amy hide out? I wondered. She loved books, so maybe a bookstore or library. I could easily imagine her huddled between tall shelves, concealed in a public place. Or she might have gone to a museum or the mall. Also, I tried to think of friends who might have heard from Amy. She mentioned a girl named Vanessa in a recent email.

Email!

I jumped up, startled by memory. I *had* heard from Amy last night. She tried to call only I hadn't been home, and she'd left a message. She'd told me to check my email, only I'd been thinking about Josh and had completely forgotten.

It took only a few minutes to power up my computer, connect online, and start scrolling through my messages. When I found the one from Amy, I clicked on it.

Hey Fave Sis,
U won't believe what Ashley did! Totally hateful!
I REFUSE TO LIVE WITH HER!!
So I'm moving 2 live with U. I got enough $$ for a
bus ticket to Lodi. Can U pick me up? Email ASAP!
C U tomorrow. Luv Amy

I read the message one more time, blaming my-
self for not checking my email sooner. She'd sent
this last night and could already be at the bus sta-
tion, waiting for me. I was a terrible sister! She was
so young and vulnerable. If anything bad happened
to her, it would be my fault.

I had to get to her—*fast!*

Grabbing my purse, which contained a spare
set of keys to Nona's car, I raced out of my room
and down the stairs. I glanced at Nona's shut office
door, tempted to confide in her. But then she'd
worry and that might trigger another memory lapse.
I couldn't risk her health. It would be much better
to bring Amy home, then we'd explain everything to
Nona. If I told Nona now, she'd want to drive to the
bus station herself and make me stay home. After
her driving experience this morning, that was *not* a
good idea.

After leaving a note explaining where I was, I
quietly left the house.

As I turned the engine of Nona's car I heard a crunch of gravel. Before I could move, someone jerked open my car door. Dominic stood there, scowling, his arms folded across his chest.

"Where do you think you're going?" he demanded.

His attitude pissed me off, and I snapped, "None of your business."

"Keeping you alive is my business."

"I'm fine, but my sister might not be."

"Amy?" he guessed, his tone softening.

I nodded. "I have to go look for her at the bus station."

"Forget it." He kept a firm grip on the door. "You're not going anywhere."

"But Amy needs me!" I exclaimed, then quickly told him about Mom's call and Amy's email. "She's only ten and traveling alone. Don't try to stop me."

"Okay—I won't," he said in a surprisingly agreeable tone.

"Thank you," I said in relief.

"But I'm driving—and you'd better call your mother."

I pursed my lips, knowing arguing would only waste time. So I shot him a furious glare, then agreed. I followed him to his truck, climbed inside, and pulled out my cell phone. I did *not* want to talk to Mom, but I did it anyway. And when I heard the tearful relief in her voice, I was glad I called.

Dominic and I didn't say much on the way to Lodi. I resented how he'd pushed me around, yet was thankful for his support. I'd never been to the bus station, but knew where it was because it was close to my favorite movie theatre. Fortunately, Dominic knew the way. The parking lot was full, but we snagged a close spot as another car was leaving.

Before Dominic shut off the engine, I was out of my seat belt and racing toward the station. A large family sat outside on a bench, luggage towering as tall as the little kids, and some guys in uniforms with military haircuts leaned against a wall. I rushed past them and entered the building.

But there was no sign of Amy, and when I checked the schedule I discovered her bus wasn't due in for over an hour. So I plopped down on a bench next to a group of elderly women all wearing blue-and-white bowling shirts. Dominic stood near the door, his gaze watchful.

I leaned my head back and closed my eyes, giving into weariness. I dozed in and out, looking up whenever a bus arrival was announced, then closing my eyes again when it was a false alarm.

Time passed. I stirred a few times, then drifted back to sleep. When I felt a gentle shaking, I looked up to find Dominic beside me with his hand on my shoulder. "Her bus just pulled in," he told me.

"Thanks." I blinked, then sat up straighter.

"She'll come in through that door," he said, stepping away from me. My shoulder tingled from where his hand had touched it. But there wasn't time to think about this. A rush of people poured into the station and there was my sister.

"Amy!" I shouted.

"Sabine!" she cried out joyfully.

We both ran, meeting with a fierce hug.

"I am so glad to see you!" I cried, reaching out with my finger to a tangled strand of brown hair on her forehead.

"I was afraid you wouldn't be here."

"I almost wasn't. This is the stupidest thing you've ever done."

"No way!" She sounded proud and not at all contrite. "This will show Ashley! She was wrong about my being dull. You wouldn't catch her skipping school and running away."

"You scared everyone!" I said sternly. "Mom is sick with worry."

"You talked to *her!*" Amy shot me an accusing look. "Did you tell her where I was?"

"I had to or she would have called the police."

"I don't care. I'd rather get handcuffed and taken to jail than go back."

"Take my advice and skip the cuffs," I said with a rueful glance at my bruised wrist. Then more seriously, I asked, "Why did you run away? Whatever Ashley did couldn't be that bad."

"Worse!" Her face twisted into fury. "I hate her."

"Tell me about it outside," I said, raising my voice over the noise. Nearby a family reunion seemed to be going on with lots of hugging and exclamations.

Dominic came over, smiling at Amy as he offered to carry her bags. "Wait here and I'll get the truck," he told us. The truck wasn't parked that far, so I guessed he was tactfully leaving us alone so we could talk privately.

"What happened?" I asked, sitting beside my sister on a wooden bench.

"Yesterday I was in my room reading, when Ashley burst in." Amy's lips puckered. "She didn't knock—she never does. Then she tells me to put down my book and hang out with her. I ask why isn't she with one of her zillion friends. She says they're all busy. So I tell her I'm busy, too."

"Why did you say that?"

"'Cause I hate being last choice. She never has time for me when I'm bored, so why should I drop everything to do what she wants?"

"You used to be inseparable," I said sadly.

"And you used to live with us. Things change."

I nodded sadly. Then I listened while she described what happened next. Ashley could be the sweetest person in the world—as long as she got what she wanted. Amy's refusal lit her fuse. She stomped over to the bed and snatched Amy's book.

"It was a rare copy of *Discovery at Dragon's Mouth* in a mint dust jacket," Amy added indignantly. "I yelled at her to give it back, but she waved it in the air and refused. I lunged for it, only I missed the book and hit Ashley. She's such a drama queen, she screamed that I tried to kill her. Well I had to get my book and lunged for it. She jerked back as I grabbed it—then there was the awful sound of paper ripping! I went crazy and started pounding on her. Then we were on the carpet, totally going at it, when Mom rushed in."

"Oh, no!" My hand flew to my mouth.

"When Mom saw that Ashley's nose was bleeding, she freaked. She wouldn't even listen to me. And . . . And she didn't care that my book jacket was ru-ruined." Amy covered her face, sobbing.

I held her close, smoothing her hair and aching with sadness. What had happened to my family? My sisters used to fight—sometimes with me—but never like this. Ashley had a quick temper, but was easy to reason with once she calmed down. Amy held anger in like a corked bottle, simmering in silence until I made her open up and talk about her feelings.

"Let's get out of here," I told Amy. "We'll go to Nona's."

She wiped her eyes and nodded numbly.

Dominic was waiting by his truck. He came around and opened the door. I stepped up inside when there was a screech of tires. Turning around, I stared at my mother's car.

"Oh, no," Amy whimpered, clutching tight to me, her palms sweaty.

"It'll be okay," I told her. But I wasn't so sure. Dad may be the lawyer in the family, but not even he was a match for Mom when she was angry. Although usually I was the one in trouble. I felt protective of

Amy, and was determined to defend her. I braced myself for an ugly scene.

But Mom took one look at Amy, and started crying. No shouting or criticizing; she simply stretched out her arms and rushed for my sister. The passenger door of her car opened and Ashley stepped out, tears streaming down her face too. She apologized to Amy, adding that she'd searched on-line and ordered another copy of the book she'd ruined. This made Amy start crying. Then the three were all sniffling and hugging.

I stood on the outside looking in. Like I wasn't part of my own family. A knot formed in my throat, and I turned to get into the truck with Dominic. I didn't fit in here with the happy reunion.

"Wait, Sabine." It was Mom, leaving the girls and coming after me.

Uncertain, I turned toward her. "What?"

"I just wanted to thank you," she said, her eyes bright with emotion.

"Well . . ." I shifted on the pavement. "You're welcome."

"You acted so quickly, displaying amazing maturity.

"When Ashley confessed about what really happened, I felt awful," she admitted in a weary tone. "I was terrified I'd never see Amy again. But then you called and I drove like a crazy woman to get here. Thank goodness she's safe! I am so grateful."

Then my mother—who wasn't very demonstrative—hugged me.

I stiffened at first, then relaxed and hugged back.

A while later, tears were dried and my mother and sisters climbed in Mom's car to head back to San Jose.

"Come visit soon, Sabine. We have a lot to discuss," Mom said with a meaningful look. I wasn't sure exactly what she meant, but it felt good to be wanted, so I nodded.

Then they drove away, and I joined Dominic at his truck.

"Thanks for waiting," I told him as I opened the passenger door.

"Couldn't just leave you here—it's a long walk back."

"I'd never make it," I said with a weary sigh.

His teasing look changed to concern. "You okay?"

"Exhausted—but feeling good."

"Problems all solved?" he asked.

"Yeah. Amy doesn't hate Ashley anymore. And Mom was amazingly decent."

"She loves you," he said simply.

"I guess so." I smiled, a bit surprised to realize this was true.

I reached around for my seat belt. As I turned, I noticed a flash of movement from the backseat. My first thought was that one of Dominic's animal friends had hitched a ride with us. But then I looked over the seat—and saw a shimmering glass globe with rainbow colors glowing from inside.

Totally, absolutely, completely impossible!

Yet it was here with us.

The witch ball.

26

Dominic reacted with equal shock when he looked in the back seat. We both were like statues, frozen with our mouths open, making no move to touch the witchy glass ball.

Finally Dominic spoke, "It can't be!"

"But it is," I said in a hushed whisper, my fingers knotted around the seat belt. "What are we going to do?"

"What we should have done days ago," he said with fierce resolve. "Smash it."

I shuddered, but realized this was the best solution. Hortense was challenging us and we had to stop her. I listened for any advice from Opal and had a strong sense that she would support whatever I decided to do.

"All right," I told Dominic. "Destroy it. But not here in a public place."

He nodded. "Better do it at the farm."

"Okay. But get it away from me."

"I'll stow it in the back."

"Thanks," I said, sagging against my seat.

I swiveled to look as he walked around to the backseat and carefully lifted the ball, which had stopped glowing. Without the menacing glow, the ball looked as harmless as a light bulb. But I knew better and shuddered.

Only after the ball was locked in the silver metal container in the bed of the truck did I breathe a sigh of relief. Locked away. And soon it would be destroyed.

A minute later, Dominic climbed into the truck and started up the engine.

As we left the bus station, Dominic and I decided to wrap the ball securely then smash it with a hammer. We had to do it in a way that left no fragments for Hortense to cling to. Complete obliteration. Then we'd perform a banishing ceremony and exorcise the ghost forever.

With this decided, our conversation switched to Nona. Dominic was eager to get home and check his phone messages. "There's a good chance this guy called about the silver charms. I think he'll be able to help us find another one."

"That would be so great."

"Three charms might be enough to locate the remedy book."

"But what condition will the book be in after all this time?" I worried.

"We could have it restored," he suggested with a glance in his rearview mirror.

"If it's ruined, nothing can restore it."

"From what I know of Agnes, she was too sharp to leave the book in an unsafe place. I figure she chose an airtight container and buried it by a landmark or building that would withstand time."

"But this much time?" I sank back in the seat, feeling weighed down by so many worries. "This quest seems so hopeless."

"Only if you give up hope."

"I am hoping, with all my heart."

"All of it?" he asked with a deep glance at me.

His tone held heavy meaning, and my emotions did a funny leap. The way he looked at me made me less lonely. Like he was someone I could trust.

But I trusted Josh, too. Only he'd never trust me again, and I'd have to accept that we were over. Maybe in time he'd forgive me and we could be friends. But nothing would ever be the same.

Things were changing with Dominic, too. And maybe it wasn't such a bad thing. There was something about him that intrigued me. I tried to act like I wasn't aware of him, sneaking glances through the corners of my eyes. Strong features, sandy brown hair that had grown a bit long so a strand curled at the base of his neck, and a mouth that would be hard as nails or soft as a feather. His eyes pooled with long-ago pain and future promises. And I wondered what we would be like together . . .

He seemed to know I was watching him, and his mouth tilted into a grin.

Then he glanced back at the road—and the grin switched to horror.

"NO!" he shouted.

In a flash I saw the cow standing in the road, its eyes wide and reflecting. Frozen, dead center in our path.

"HOLD ON!" Dominic shouted, slamming on the brakes, yanking the wheel and swerving wildly.

Everything happened so fast—screeching tires, spinning us out of control, careening across the lane, spinning wildly, then plunging over a ditch, rolling over and over. Breaking glass, a crashing explosion in my head.

Then the witch ball's final prediction came true.

I died.

27

It wasn't bad being dead.

Light and peaceful—except for a disjointed sense of confusion. I floated above the ground, without feeling cold or fear. I could see Dominic's truck—or what was left of his truck—smashed and tilted on its side with two wheels spinning. The metal container in the back was unhinged, its top flung yards away onto the pavement, surrounded by scattered shards of glass that glittered like fallen stars underneath a street light. And nearby a cow plodded back to its pasture.

In the driver's seat I saw Dominic slumped and unconscious. It occurred to me that I should be more upset, or at least scared. All I felt was a distant sense of concern, which passed quickly. I knew he was alive and he'd be okay. A dazzling light surrounded me and I was buoyant and joyful. I had places to go and people to see, and I was eager to go on—

"Not yet, Sabine," I heard a familiar voice, and when I looked beside me there was Opal. Not just the vague black-haired face I usually saw in my mind, but she was real and alive like me.

"Opal!" I held out my arms and seemed to float into hers. When she held me, wonderful sensations multiplied and everything was perfect. No worries and fears, nothing except love.

"Are you all right?" she asked me.

"Of course! I've never felt better."

"It's only beginning," she said with wry smile. "Are you sure this is what you want?"

"Of course!" Brilliant light filled me and I felt myself lifting up. I could no longer see the truck or

Dominic. But somehow that seemed wrong, and a wave of confusion dragged me down. "What's happenning? I'm confused . . ."

"It's always confusing at first," she said gently.

"Is this the other side?"

"Not yet."

"Am I dead?"

"For the moment." She held my hands and peered into my face. "Is that what you want?"

"I'm happy being with you," I said simply.

"Is that enough? What about your earth family and friends?"

"I'll see them eventually."

"True. But what about her?" She pointed off into a gray area of clouds where a shadowy figure stood apart and alone.

My overwhelming joy dimmed a little as I recognized the witch ball ghost. She stood alone in a haze of bleak nothingness, pitiful and cut off from any world.

"Why doesn't she come to us?" I asked.

"She's too afraid."

"But there's nothing to be afraid of here."

"We know that, but she doesn't. She won't talk to me, but she might listen to you. Do you want to go to her?"

"And leave all this?" I gestured around, not at anything solid but more an essence of pure joy. Beyond the horizon, I saw dim shapes of smiling people, waving and eager to greet me. And I longed to go to them, to have all questions answered and rejoice in homecoming.

Yet the pathetic old-fashioned ghost who clung to a lifeless piece of glass tugged at my heart. The witch ball was her only home. I couldn't just abandon her.

I found myself drawing away from Opal, into a gray void. The happy feelings faded and I was left with a stark aching pain worse than anything I'd ever experienced. As if my very heart had been ripped out.

"Hortense," I called out, struggling against panic and fear. "Will you talk to me?"

She loomed closer, her hands like bird claws clutching her faded dark skirt. Her face was lined, as if everything alive had been drained from her.

"Leave me be," she spoke, turning away.

But I moved around to face her. "Please, listen. You can't go on like this."

"What concern is it of yours?" she demanded in sharp suspicion. "You have done nothing but cause me problems, stealing my witch ball and using your evil magic to thwart me."

"I never meant to hurt you."

"Your mistake. I warned you that you would die, and it has come to pass. You were foolish to challenge my powers. Now you will suffer as I have."

"But I'm not suffering. I'm happy," I said, offering her a smile. "I'd like to help you find happiness too."

"I need no assistance, only to be left alone."

"No one deserves to be this alone," I said, gesturing to the vast, empty grayness around her. "Don't you have family that you'd like to be with?"

"Family?" Her lips twisted. "Those that professed their love left me. My parents and siblings took ill with the plague. I was forced into a loveless marriage. The only bright spot was a child I bore, but he died hours after birth. When I failed to conceive again, my husband abandoned me."

"I'm sorry."

"Save your pity and be on your way."

I felt a tugging to return to the light, where I knew I'd be met by love. And I wondered who would meet Hortense.

The answer was suddenly clear. "Hortense, you have to go to your family."

"Do you not hear properly, girl?" she snapped. "I have not kin."

"But you do . . . on the other side. They're all waiting for you."

She frowned. "But tis not possible."

"You may have forgotten them, but they never gave up on you. Your parents, brothers and sisters, and your son. They're all waiting for you."

"My little babe?" Her wrinkles softened. "Can't be so, not when he barely breathed a few breaths before his tiny body went still."

"But he loved you for that short time, as much as you loved him," I said, knowing this with a strong certainty. "All you have to do to be with him is go into the light."

"He's waiting . . . for me?" Her voice was hushed.

"Yes. He's already been waiting a long time. Don't make him wait any longer." I pointed towards the brilliant light which now seemed close enough to touch. "Go to him."

"My son," she murmured. "It can't be so."

"But it is. He's reaching out for you."

"Yes . . . yes! I can see him." Hortense's face glowed and slowly she held out her arms. Then she moved forward. I stood aside, watching her transform; the wrinkles faded to soft luminous skin. Even her drab skirt seemed brighter and her gray hair darkened to a lovely chestnut brown. Light and love enveloped her like a sweet fog. And the last thing I saw was her arms upraised and a child's voice calling out, "Mama!"

Then Opal was by my side and I was overcome by dizziness. She held me tight, whispering that I had a choice, too. When I looked down I saw the mangled truck, the wheels still spinning. There was a strong smell of diesel. And I thought of everyone I loved—Nona, my mother, father, sisters, and friends.

Light faded and I was being sucked into a tornado. There was heaviness, enormous pain, and everything was black.

"Hold on," I heard a voice above me.

Warm hands grasped me gently, lifting my head. I felt warm lips on mine. Blowing air, expanding my chest.

"Breathe, damn it!"

Dominic. I thought. *It's Dominic.*

More pressure on my mouth and a pressure on my chest. The pain was so severe, I backed off and started to float away.

"Sabine!" I saw Dominic's face over mine. "Stay with me . . . I won't let you go!"

He held tighter, the mouth-to-mouth he'd been using to save me deepening into a warm kiss. He caressed my hair, his touch gentle, not letting go. I clung to him, kissing him back, giving into tingling desire. Sinking into him, floating in sweet emotions.

I whispered his name, other sensations heightened—cold gravel underneath me on hard ground, stinging, cuts on my skin, and a growing ache in my head. Everything blurred and I trembled. Except for the warmth on my lips, the rest of my body exploded with pain.

There was the sound of sirens and I saw red and blue flashing lights. I thought wistfully of the bright lights I left behind, the homecoming I didn't join.

Then I blacked out.

28

"Saturday," the nurse told me when I woke up and asked what day it was.

"What?" I thought I was yelling, but the sound that came from my throat was only a small frog croak. My vision was foggy, but after blinking, I could see I was in a hospital room: white walls, white sheets, and a garden of brilliant flowers on a nearby shelf.

"Sabine honey," I heard my grandmother's voice. She stood up from a corner chair and rushed over to my bedside. "You're back."

"Was I . . . I gone?" I whispered.

She gave me an odd look. "Don't you remember?"

It seemed strange, this question coming from her. But I knew what she meant, although my memory of Opal, Hortense, and the others was already fading; like a dream slipping away upon waking. I just nodded.

She told me it was very early on Saturday, so she was my only visitor. "But it's been crowded with everyone who cares about you. Your doctor joked about selling tickets. Your parents and sisters had to go back home but will return later. And your friends should show up soon."

I had so many questions but Nona had moved over to the shelf with flowers and was reading off the "get well soons" and other messages. When she came to a small, glass vase with wildflowers, she withdrew an attached envelope and handed it to me.

"This came from Dominic. He acted quite mysterious, telling me not to open it until you were awake, and said it was a surprise for both of us."

I pushed myself farther up against the pillow and weakly ran my thumbnail against the sealed flap. I lifted out a folded paper. It said: Thirds is a charm. And it was signed simply "D."

I was puzzled, until I realized there was something else in the envelope. When I looked inside, I gave an excited cry. Then I lifted up a tiny, silver charm—very old, finely hand-crafted—and shaped like a tiny fish.

Nona was thrilled, full of hope that the remedy book would be found soon. And I was thrilled, too, for many reasons.

I wanted to ask which friends had come, flashing back to that kiss with Dominic. I couldn't pretend nothing was between us. He'd breathed life into me; a deep kiss that told me more than I wanted to know. Yet it filled me with joy, too. And I had to admit, finally to myself, that I enjoyed it.

So what did it all mean? Was there something serious between us? We were different, but he understood about my gift and I couldn't deny the chemistry beween us. My relationship with Josh was over anyway. He'd been angry with me for standing him up and Evan would have told him about my weirdness by now, so he wouldn't want anything to do with me. Without Josh, school would be lonely. But with Dominic, after school could prove very interesting.

My head started to throb again, and soon a nurse appeared with pain pills. I sipped some juice, swallowed the pills, then fell back asleep.

When I woke again, Nona was gone. But I had another visitor—the last person I expected to see.

"Josh! You . . . here?" I said hoarsely, surely I must've been hallucinating.

He stood up from the uncomfortable-looking plastic chair, and came over to my side. "Sabine! I've been so worried."

"You have?"

"What do you expect? You're my girl." He reached out to squeeze my hand. "I freaked when I heard about the accident. And I felt terrible for treating you so rough. I didn't know about your sister running away. I should have trusted that you wouldn't have ditched me without a good reason. Can you forgive me?"

"Me? Forgive you?"

"I jumped to the wrong conclusion. Thank God you're okay." He reached out to squeeze my hand. "And we're together. That's all that matters."

"But . . ." My throat tightened, so I took a sip of water. "But Evan . . . didn't he . . . tell you?"

"Oh, that." Josh rolled his eyes. "Yeah, he showed me a newspaper clipping and told me some stuff about you."

"Are you mad?"

"You bet I am! At all those stupid people at your school—and at Evan. No wonder you kept this a secret. It must have hurt."

"You don't . . . mind?"

"It's not your fault that other people are ignorant. I know what it's like to lose someone close—you want to blame someone. But those people had no right making up those lies about you."

"Lies?"

"Yeah, sure. Only an idiot would believe you have the power to predict the future."

"Yeah." I laughed shakily. "It's crazy."

"Although right now I can predict a great future for us." He looked down at me with such a tender expression, my heart swelled with gratitude.

Then the door opened and Manny and Thorn burst in.

Josh said he'd leave so they could visit for a while, but he promised to come back later. Then he bent down to gently kiss me. A very sweet kiss that should have made me feel wonderful. Instead I ached with guilt for betraying him . . . and an uncertain longing.

I laid back against my pillow, weary yet glad to be alive and surrounded by friends.

I listened while Manny and Thorn filled me in on everything that happened since my accident. Thorn had indeed found K.C.'s car, only it had been stripped and most of his stuff was gone. So Thorn had taken him home to her minister mother—and he was staying with them while he sorted out his life.

Penny-Love and Nona showed up next. Penny-Love was excited to start working with Nona, and I could tell Nona was relieved to have someone help with her business. Nona didn't say much, just held my hand, while Penny-Love went on with school gossip and the newest on her latest love. I didn't have the heart to tell her Jacques was really plain Jack and might be dealing drugs. Maybe later . . .

By the time they left, I was so exhausted, I only ate part of my bland hospital lunch, then sank into a deep sleep.

It was almost dark out my window when my eyes opened. The visitor chairs were empty. I was alone. And I found myself wondering why Dominic hadn't come to see me. Thinking about him brought a sudden insight. When he thought I was dying, he'd told me he loved me. In fact, according to the doctor, I had died for a few seconds. All the predictions *had* come true.

But now what would happen? Josh was still my boyfriend—then there was Dominic. I couldn't believe two great guys cared about me—and I had absolutely no idea what to do about it.

There was a knock on my door, and I was surprised since visiting hours had ended. I called out a weak "come in." It was my mother.

"Good evening, Sabine," she said, her words formal but there was a warmth in her tone that was new.

"Hi, Mom. Are Dad and the girls here?"

She shook her head. "Not this time, but they'll be here tomorrow."

"Good."

She pulled a chair close to my bed. "I purposely came alone, because there's something important I want to tell you."

"What?"

"I've done some soul-searching lately. The shock of Amy running away, and then your accident, made me rethink a lot of things."

"I'm fine now," I told her. "I'm bruised and cut up, but nothing serious. You don't have to worry about me."

"But I do worry. I'm sorry for everything, Sabine. I realize now that I made a horrible mistake."

"Mistake?" I asked, puzzled by the anguish in her voice.

"Yes, dear." She reached out and grasped my hand. "That's why I've made a serious decision about you."

"What decision?"

"I was wrong to make you leave home. It's time I made amends." She peered close into my face and tightened her hold on my hand. "Sabine, as soon as you're well enough to travel, you're moving back to San Jose."

The End

THE SEER

Sword Play

The following is an unedited excerpt from The Seer 4, *Sword Play* by Linda Joy Singleton.

1

Waking up to find a cute guy sitting on your bed might be a dream come true for some girls.

But not me.

Especially when the guy was dead—and some people think I killed him.

Normally ghosts don't scare me. Coming from a long line of psychics, I'd been weaned on Ghosts, Spirits, and Angels 101. I've had visions of the future and long chatty conversations with my spirit guide. But this was different. This was Kip.

Seeing him so alive and real—only six months after his death was beyond freaky. Terror sliced through me like a sharp blade.

"Go away!" I shouted, then ducked underneath my pillow, my eyes shut tightly and my heart pounding furiously.

Please let this be a bad dream. Yeah, that must be it. I was having a nightmare or maybe a reaction to the pain medication. I remembered falling asleep, relieved to be out of the hospital and back in my own familiar quilted bed. After surviving a deadly road accident, it was logical that I'd dream about car crashes—including the tragedy that would always haunt me. But that was all in the past. I mean, this could not be happening. No way was Kip Hurst in my room.

But when I peeked out, there he was, decked out in his #17 football jersey (which was odd since he'd died in a formal prom tux). Energy flickered around him, making his face seem unnaturally pale while his legs were so transparent that when he stood it looked like he was floating over my bed. A football appeared in his hand and he spun it on his fingertip, grinning at me in that arrogant way I always detested.

"Go away!" I tried again.

With a tilt of his head, he regarded me with wry curiosity.

"Get out of here!"

He tossed the ball so high it disappeared into my dark ceiling.

I stared up, waiting for the football—and my own sanity—to return. Long moments stretched on in eerie silence; then the ball slowly sailed into his hand. Only his energy flickered and his hand wasn't there. The football balanced on its pointy end in empty air. I pinched myself, just to check if I was, in fact, dreaming. Ouch! Definitely not a dream.

Kip's hand may have vanished and his legs were see-through, but his grin flashed with a mega-watt cocky attitude. Clearly he was not going away.

Gathering my blankets around me, I scooted upright in bed and faced this ghost from my past. Kip had been a star football player with major league expectations and he'd also been a three-time homecoming king.

At my old school, Arcadia High, where sports ruled and had more funding than any other department, Kip was truly royalty.

I wasn't one of Kip's fans. It just seemed to me that jocks were overrated. I mean, what was so great about pummeling players on a field? I hadn't even known Kip, except by reputation . . . until The Vision.

Then why was he here so many months later?

Unless he blamed me . . .

I swallowed hard, then forced out the question I knew I had to ask. "What do you want?"

I could barely make out his shadowy hand pointing directly at me.

To write to the author

If you wish to contact the author, please write to the author in care of Llewellyn Worldwide, and we will forward your letter. Both the author and publisher appreciate hearing from you and learning of your enjoyment of this book. Llewellyn Worldwide cannot guarantee that every letter written to the author can be answered, but all will be forwarded. Please write to:

Linda Joy Singleton
℅ Llewellyn Worldwide
2143 Wooddale Drive, Dept. 0-7387-0821-6
Woodbury, MN 55125-2989

Please enclose a self-addressed stamped envelope, or one dollar to cover costs. If outside U.S.A., enclose international postal reply coupon.

Many of Llewellyn's authors have Web sites with additional information and resources. For more information, please visit our Web site at:

http://www.llewellyn.com

Llewellyn Worldwide does not participate in, endorse, or have any authority or responsibility concerning private business transactions between our authors and the public.

what do you like to read?

Llewellyn would love to know what kinds of books you are looking for but just can't seem to find. Fantasy, witchy, occult, science fiction, or just plain scary—what do you want to read? What types of books speak specifically to you? If you have ideas, suggestions, or comments, please write us at:

ideas@llewellyn.com

Llewellyn Publications
Attn: YA, Acquisitions
2143 Wooddale Drive
Woodbury, MN 55125-2989
1-800-T   6)